Don't g

Penn rose from
the mead

Poor fe
boy, looki
bloody an
Penn saw
little. He was breathing!

Penn knelt and put his face low to the ground, looking into the young man's face.

"Young man, can you hear me?"

The boy murmured softly. His eyelids fluttered.

"You're hurt badly, my friend," Penn said. "I'll not lie to you about that. I don't know if I can help you, but I'll try."

"Parlee . . ."—the young man's voice was the weakest of whispers—". . . robbers, killers . . . in Marrowbone . . . in Marrowbone . . ."

"Please," Penn said, grasping the young man's hand. His body stiffened, the hand squeezed tight, then relaxed utterly as it slipped from Penn's grasp. . . .

Down to Marrowbone

Judson Gray

A SIGNET BOOK

SIGNET
Published by New American Library, a division of
Penguin Putnam Inc., 375 Hudson Street,
New York, New York 10014, U.S.A.
Penguin Books Ltd, 27 Wrights Lane,
London W8 5TZ, England
Penguin Books Australia Ltd, Ringwood,
Victoria, Australia
Penguin Books Canada Ltd, 10 Alcorn Avenue,
Toronto, Ontario, Canada M4V 3B2
Penguin Books (N.Z.) Ltd, 182–190 Wairau Road,
Auckland 10, New Zealand

Penguin Books Ltd, Registered Offices:
Harmondsworth, Middlesex, England

First published by Signet, an imprint of New American Library,
a division of Penguin Putnam Inc.

First Printing, November 2000
10 9 8 7 6 5 4 3 2 1

Copyright © Cameron Judd, 2000
All rights reserved

Ⓤ REGISTERED TRADEMARK—MARCA REGISTRADA

Printed in the United States of America

PUBLISHER'S NOTE
This is a work of fiction. Names, characters, places, and incidents either
are the product of the author's imagination or are used fictitiously, and
any resemblance to actual persons, living or dead, business establish-
ments, events or locales is entirely coincidental.

BOOKS ARE AVAILABLE AT QUANTITY DISCOUNTS WHEN USED TO PROMOTE PRODUCTS
OR SERVICES. FOR INFORMATION PLEASE WRITE TO PREMIUM MARKETING DIVISION, PEN-
GUIN PUTNAM INC., 375 HUDSON STREET, NEW YORK, NEW YORK 10014.

To Sam Tanner

PART 1

McCutcheon

Chapter One

The lightning flash brought Jake Penn to his feet so fast he bumped his head on the ceiling of the low, shallow cavern in which he'd taken shelter.

He approached the mouth of the cave and peered out into the darkness, violent with rain. A second lightning flash confirmed that his senses hadn't fooled him.

Indeed, in the brief flare of light, he was sure he saw an entire cabin wash over the nearby waterfall with a rending crash. And he was almost sure a human body had been hanging halfway out of one of the cabin's windows when it did.

Without a moment's pause, Penn plunged into the driving rain. He wore a mackinaw, but his hat remained back in the cave, forgotten in his haste. He ignored the rain hammering his shoulders, soaking his hair, and gushing down inside his collar.

He ran to the stream's edge, which was much closer now to the cave than it had been an hour before. It was no longer a stream at all, but a wild and growing river, alive with rapids and debris that shot along its surface at dangerous speeds.

The lightning soon revealed the ruins of the cabin in the water. What remained was falling apart fast, logs turning and swirling, wrenching, grinding and splintering.

Penn cupped his hands around his mouth. "Anybody there?" His voice, usually rich and sonorous, sounded unnaturally feeble against the combined roars of the storm and the overflowing river.

He waited for an answer but received none.

Another series of lightning flashes illuminated the rushing water. The cabin was completely torn apart now, loose logs jamming up where the stream narrowed, forming something that looked like an oversized beaver dam, causing the water to pool even faster beneath the falls.

He'd seen this all in those few moments of light, but he hadn't seen any sign of a human in the water. Perhaps he hadn't really seen a body in that window at all.

"Ho, there!" Penn yelled again, just to be sure. "Is there anybody out there to hear me?"

Again, there was no reply. There was also no

lightning for nearly half a minute. The rain pummeled down harder, the hardest rain Penn had ever experienced. It fell almost like a solid sheet of liquid, striking so hard it strung the skin not covered by his thick mackinaw.

He was nearly convinced now that he'd only imaged seeing someone in that window. There was another possibility: There really *had* been a body in the window, but whoever it was, was surely dead now, or dying, maybe pinned beneath the water by some of those jammed-up logs.

If so, there was nothing he could do. In this darkness and this pounding storm, it would be impossible for him to hope to find a person in such a desperate situation.

Penn supposed the cabin had been some old streamside miner's hut that had been dislodged by floodwaters somewhere up the mountain. It even might have washed down all the way from the little mining town of Millrace—the place he'd been heading when nightfall had fore-stalled him.

Penn had been asleep in the little cavern when the storm hit. His horse had been frightened away—a very bad turn of luck—but at least he'd lost nothing else. His saddle, bags, and beloved Winchester rifle were safely stowed in the cave.

He'd been hopeful he'd be able to find his

horse again come morning. Now he wasn't sure. A storm this fierce might drive the horse halfway across the country.

Lightning struck a tree a mile away. Light and fire shot toward the sky; thunder resounded like a cannon's blast. By the light, Penn spotted a human form, floating motionless and facedown in the water.

He cast off his mackinaw and plunged into the water, dodging debris, fighting the current's best efforts to pull him under. Hampered by all his clothes, he struggled to swim toward the place he'd last seen the body, wondering if all this valiant effort was wasted. The body floated like that of a dead man.

A fragment of the cabin struck Penn and knock him sideways. His feet left the stream bottom and for a moment he was submerged. Finally, his head came back up and he bobbed along, out of control, dragged by the torrential flow toward the tangling log jam at the bottleneck farther down the stream.

He struck the logs, steadied himself against them, and found a handhold. The current slammed against him, throwing him against the log jam.

Something bulky nudged him from behind. He groped at the object and realized that the floating body had washed up against him.

Penn clung to the log jam with one arm and snagged the floating man by the collar with the other, dragging him close. He was able to get an arm firmly wrapped around the man's neck. With effort, Penn heaved the body over so it floated on its back, face skyward and nose out of the water. The eyes were tightly closed, the mouth slack.

Penn couldn't tell for sure, but he thought he felt the man move a little, sucking in air.

"Keep on living, friend," he said. "Just keep on living a little bit longer."

The tangled logs made threatening creaks that indicated the whole heap of them might give way at any moment. Penn desperately tried to keep a grip on the man trapped in his arm while maintaining his balance against the current. If not for the natural buoyancy of the limp body, he doubted he could have kept hold at all.

Penn maneuvered along the wall of logs, inching closer to the bank, finding occasional toeholds. He made slow progress, hampered by his burden.

Lightning revealed a big log washing over the falls, caught in the charging current. It hurtled toward the two men like a battering ram, but was deflected at the last moment when it struck against a midstream boulder.

Penn paused a moment to let his heart start up again.

"Come on, friend," he said to his silent companion. "If you've got any senses or any strength left in you at all, now's the time to put them to use and help me. I fear I'll drop you."

But the unmoving man remained unresponsive.

Penn pushed toward the bank. Abruptly his feet found firmer ground. Straining, he pulled the sodden and unmoving figure onto the bank.

He laid the unconscious man facedown and began bellowing the water from his lungs. The senseless man heaved suddenly, gasping, but did not fully come to.

Penn pulled the young man to the cave, out of the storm, then plunged briefly into the deluge again to recover his mackinaw. He returned to the little cavern and set out to discover just what kind of human flotsam he'd just salvaged.

Penn built up the fire again, filling the cavern with flickering light. He pulled a half-consumed cigar from his pocket, wanting a smoke, then laughed at himself and tossed the thoroughly soaked stogie away. The storm howled on outside, gusts of wind making the coals flare.

He rolled the rescued man over onto his back. Leaning over, he studied the fellow closely.

He was a grown man, though young. In his

twenties, Penn guessed. He had no whiskers beyond the few days' growth of a man on the trail. Thick dark hair, well-shaped features, tanned skin, but so far the man was still protected sufficiently by youthfulness to stave off the leathering that was the eventual fate of every sunbaked Westerner.

Peeling back an eyelid revealed blue eyes, maybe gray. Hard to be sure in the faint glow of the firelight. The man's eyes were rolled up in his head, showing mostly the whites.

No obvious wounds or bruises marked the man's face. Penn figured this young buck was probably thought quite handsome by all the young ladies.

He looked closer at the face, reaching a finger out and tracing the dim line of a jagged scar that ran down across the man's left temple toward his jaw.

Penn shifted his angle of view a few times, studying that scar, and the face as a whole.

Something about it was familiar, something nagging inexplicably at his mind.

Penn tried to make sense of it, but couldn't figure it out.

Turning away, he added a little more wood to the fire, then scooted the young man into a position to let the heat better reach and dry him. Though it was summer, evenings were cool in the

Rockies, made cooler yet because of the howling storm.

Wondering if the unconscious man might have any identification on him, he began patting him down, searching through the pockets. He didn't find anything helpful except one faded, water-logged letter. The ink with which it was written was far from waterfast, most of the words smeared and unreadable. The fragment of the name of the recipient remained legible, though.

"Cutch," Penn read.

Penn put the letter back in the unconscious man's pocket and settled against the back wall of the cavern, his knees up, elbows folded across them, chin on hand. He stared at the supine figure, then out across the fire into the storm.

It had been a beauty of a storm, troublesome as it had proven to be. He'd loved storms ever since he was a boy in Alabama. He would sneak out on stormy nights to the loft window of the humble quarters, where he and his family had lived as slaves, to peer out at the lightning and shiver with delight at the thunder.

He eyed the unconscious man's lightly scarred temple again.

What was it that nagged at him? Why did that scar seem to be trying to remind him of something? He pondered deeply, but soon gave up the effort in frustration.

It would be dawn soon. He'd been asleep when the storm awakened him. He'd try not to fall asleep again, in case this fellow came around.

Chapter Two

The young man sat up, staring wildly at Penn, looking very addled and quite fearful. It was just beginning to grow light outside.

Penn scooted up straight, concerned by the wild glare of the revived stranger.

"Howdy," he said. "Good to see you awake."

The younger man had the look of an animal freshly trapped. He did not reply.

"You don't know me, young man," the older man said. "My name is Jake Penn. I had to fish you out of the stream over yonder a few minutes ago."

The wild eyes glared on.

"Why you staring like that? I believe you must find me interesting. What's the matter—you never seen a Negro man before?"

Penn saw no evidence that the young man had even really heard his voice.

"Do you talk?" Penn asked.

The young man lunged, an abrupt and unpredictable move. In a flash he had Penn's rifle out of its boot, lifted, and aimed at Penn's chest.

"You'll not accuse me of that I didn't do!" the young man yelled. "You'll not hang me as no horse thief! I'll not let you!"

Penn scrambled back, trying to rise, bumping his head. "Don't you shoot me!" he hollered.

The young man moved toward the opening of the cavern, but stumbled.

The rifle fired, the slug striking stone just beside Jake Penn and singing off out into the morning.

When Penn had regained his breath, he was swept by a deep fury. He had endured many things in his life, many things he would willingly endure again, if he must, but being shot at was something he could not abide. Particularly when the man he'd saved from death was the one doing the shooting, and it was his own rifle being used against him.

Penn charged with a roar, grabbed the smoking rifle by the barrel, and wrenched it from the other man's hands. He brandished it like a club and pounded the young stranger solidly in the forehead.

The fellow sank back into unconsciousness again, collapsing on the remains of the fire.

Penn rolled him off the hot coals before any damage could be done.

"I ought to leave you to roast," he said. "I don't like being shot at. And let me tell you this, too: I'm taking your sorry hide with me to Millrace, and when we get there, I'm finding the law and letting them have you. A man who'd try to shoot his own rescuer ain't fit to be free."

Penn strode slowly up the mountain, wondering if he would find anything left of the town of Millrace. Scattered down the mountainside were scraps of buildings, pieces of furniture, casks, boxes, and assorted refuse, washed down in the same flood that had sent the cabin, and the stranger he thought of as "Cutch," over the waterfall.

Penn had found his strayed horse almost immediately after leaving the cavern. It hadn't gone far despite the fierce storm, and returned to him readily when he called. He was quite relieved—it was a good horse, a valuable possession. Having it back again also solved the problem of what he was to do with his saddle, packs, and Cutch.

Cutch sat astride the horse, leaning forward over the saddlehorn. He was tied to the horse with two ropes, one bound to his wrists and looped under and around the horse's neck, another tied around his waist and similarly looped farther back. Cutch's position would have been quite uncomfortable but for the fact that he was still unconscious.

Penn was growing anxious the farther he traveled up the mountain. This was a potentially important journey he was completing. If the leads he had so painstakingly followed proved accurate, *she* would be there, in Millrace. He wondered how different she would be, and if she would know him when she saw him. He was certain he would recognize her immediately.

Cutch moaned. Penn glanced back at him, but Cutch didn't awaken. Penn wondered if he'd struck the fellow harder than he'd realized. He hoped not. Penn had no ambition to become a killer, even in self-defense. He'd fought many a fight in his day when he had to, but at the bottom of it all, Jake Penn was a peaceful, live-and-let-live sort of man.

The atmosphere warmed as the sun moved higher in the sky. It was going to be a beautiful day, it appeared. A fine day for a long-hoped-for reunion between a brother and a sister who hadn't seen each other for many a year.

Penn stopped. Two riders had just appeared before him, heading down from the direction of Millrace. One of them was black, he noticed, the other a white man with a blondish beard and a broad, ruddy face. Both rode chestnut mares and wore pistols, with rifles booted on their saddles. Neither looked particularly hostile, however.

The riders stopped, having seen Penn. They studied one another across the distance for a time. Penn wondered what the pair made of the sight of a black man with a white one tied into the saddle.

The two riders heeled their horses and began to draw closer.

Penn held silent as they came within speaking distance.

The bearded rider looked closely at Penn, then at Cutch. "Howdy," he said.

"Hello," Penn replied.

"My name's Fifer. Jack Fifer. This here with me is Johnny Bee."

"Pleased, gentlemen. My name's Jake Penn." He tossed his head slightly, indicating Cutch. "The man on the horse there is named Cutch, or something close to that."

"His name's Jim McCutcheon."

McCutcheon. As had happened when he saw that scar, Penn was gripped by the feeling that all this had a familiar quality. *McCutcheon . . .* somehow he knew that name.

"How do you know him?" Penn asked.

"Mr. Bee and I have met him before," Fifer said in a grim tone. "Jim McCutcheon is the name he gave us. Of course, I couldn't prove to you it's his real one. Men of his ilk often use many names."

"Is he dead?" asked Johnny Bee.

"No. Knocked senseless, though."

"Why's he tied on the horse?"

"To keep him from falling off."

"Looks like you've got a prisoner. Are you some kind of lawman?"

"I'm not law. But he belongs in the hands of the law. He tried to shoot me. I don't know why—I saved him from drowning."

"Drowning?" Fifer repeated, his brows lifting.

"That's right. He washed over a waterfall farther back down the mountain. He was inside a cabin at the time."

"I'll be! So that's what happened to him. We knew he'd hid somewhere. Guess he picked the wrong place."

Penn went on. "I pulled him out of the water and got some life back into him. He thanked me by taking my own rifle and trying to kill me with it. I had to pound his head and knock him cold."

"Why'd you bother to bring him with you? Why didn't you just leave him lying there?"

"It seemed to me best to turn him over to the law at Millrace."

"I see." The man glanced at his partner. "Then you're a lucky man, Mr. Penn. I'm the marshal of Millrace." He drew his horse a little closer and put out his hand to Penn in a friendly manner. "Marshal Jack Fifer, at your service. Mr. Bee here is my deputy."

Penn shook the offered hand. He had a good feeling about Fifer all at once. Not many white men would extend a hand to a black one, and not many white peace officers kept black deputies. Fifer must be a forward-thinking kind of man.

"Pleased to know you," Penn said.

"We'll take your burden off your hands now."

"Glad to give him to you. Will you need a statement from me about the shooting?"

"We already have reasons to hold him. Mc-Cutcheon there is a murderer. Killed an innocent Methodist preacher because he'd scolded him for being drunk on the street. We were in the process of chasing him down when that storm struck, and we lost him."

Penn looked back at McCutcheon, astonished. A murderer! He'd harbored a worrisome question up until now about whether McCutcheon might have shot at him by accident rather than intention. The rifle McCutcheon had snatched was sensitive on the trigger. But what he'd just heard made it easy to believe it was no accident after all.

"He said something about horse thieving when he came to, right before he shot at me," Penn said.

"He's a horse thief, too. And probably guilty of about every other crime you can think of. You're in dangerous company there, Mr. Penn."

"Gentlemen, I'm glad you came along, and I'm glad to give him over to your custody."

"Johnny, we'll have to transfer him to your horse," Fifer said to his partner, who nodded and dismounted.

"I'm heading to Millrace," Penn said. "If you want to leave him where he is to haul him back, and save the trouble of shifting him, it's fine with me."

"No, no," Fifer quickly replied. "My deputy and me have some other business to attend elsewhere before we return to town . . . or to what's left of it after the flood. It's best we keep this villain in the meanwhile, rather than leaving it to a private citizen such as yourself. We'll keep a close eye on him until we can properly lock him up. Thank heaven that damned storm at least spared the town's jail."

Penn nodded. He liked Fifer more by the moment. The man had a sincere, trust-inspiring manner. He seemed to be a marshal who took his job seriously.

Fifer spoke again. "Sir, you've done a service to the public good by bringing this scoundrel in. We'd feared he'd escaped us for good. Bad desperado, that one. You are indeed fortunate he failed to kill you. I only wish we had some sort of reward money to offer you."

Penn helped them transfer McCutcheon from his horse to that of the deputy. McCutcheon stirred and moaned, but didn't wake up. Penn wondered if he'd ever revive at all, or if he'd been hurt bad enough in his misadventures to slowly die. If McCutcheon did die, at least Penn could know that the man he'd killed had been deserving of his fate.

Penn said, "Marshal, I'd like to ask you something, if I may. I'm going to Millrace looking for a woman. My sister. Her name is Nora; what her last name would be now, I couldn't say. She may be married now."

"I'm afraid I don't know of any women of your race in Millrace, Mr. Penn," Fifer said.

Penn was crestfallen. "None at all?"

"None that I'm aware of. And I would likely know. Millrace is a small community. My deputy and I tend to become quickly aware even of travelers who come through. I believe we would know of this Nora if she had been there. But do go on and make your own investigation, if you wish." He paused, and glanced at Bee. "Tell them that the town marshal sent you."

Bee grinned, and Penn wondered why. For the first time the thought came that maybe he didn't fully grasp all that was going on here. But it was a passing thought, which took no root.

Penn took one last look at McCutcheon. The morning light illuminated that faint scar on McCutcheon's left temple, and for a moment Penn felt that same sense of something tugging at his memory, but not tugging quite hard enough.

That name McCutcheon . . . why does it seem so familiar to me?

He watched the two lawmen go off, then mounted his own horse and rode in the opposite direction, up the mountain toward the flood-ravaged mining town of Millrace.

Chapter Three

Jake Penn had never been to Millrace before, and had heard only minimal things about it. He had not expected to find much. The town was terribly damaged because of the flood, but even without that consideration, Millrace was at best a tiny, squalid farrago; a jumbled collection of huts, tents, cabins, a few stores, offices, and the like. The street, not really a street at all, was a mass of trodden mud, glistening and puddled deeply. Over all, the town reminded Penn of some of the worse gatherings of slave huts he'd seen in a childhood of bondage that was both an eternity past and as fresh as yesterday.

He dismounted and led his horse along higher and drier ground, circling around rather than riding through the town. Everywhere people were at work, cleaning up the storm's damage, some looking angry, some helpless, some resigned. All looked weary.

There were fewer people about than he'd expected. He had heard that Millrace was on the decline as a mining town, but what he saw hardly even qualified for the label "community" anymore.

Two children played at the edge of a board porch on a miner's hut, poking in the mud below the porch with sticks. A third, a younger girl more daring than the others, tightroped back and forth along the flat top board of the porch railing. Penn approached them. He'd learned that information was often best gotten from children, who bore fewer prejudices and suspicions than the typical adult, and spoke more freely.

These proved to be friendly youngsters, one of them speaking up even before Penn could say hello.

"That's a fine horse you got," the girl on the railing said. "My pa had a horse like that once, but he sold it."

"He is a fine horse. Thank you for noticing." Penn spoke to the group as a whole. "You young folks, can I ask you something?"

The mud-pokers looked at him and shrugged lightly. "Reckon you can," said the eldest.

"I came here looking for a woman I ain't seen in many years. My sister. Her name is Nora. You know any Negro women named Nora around here?"

"I don't," the boy said, not missing a step.

"Me, neither," the other mud-poker said.

"I know one," the girl said.

Penn's pulse raced. "She's here, then?"

"Not no more. Nora is gone."

"She was a Negro, like me?"

"Yes. I liked her. She was quiet, and I didn't know her much, but she was kind. She was kind of like a queen, the way she walked around real straight. I used to pretend she was a queen, sometimes, come over from Africa to find her family who was brung here by slavers."

"Where is Nora now?" Penn asked.

"I don't know. She's just gone away."

"Alone?"

"No. There's a family she was with. She worked for them, I think. She went away with them."

"Wait a minute," the eldest boy said. "I remember her now. Yeah. Nora. She was always with the family who lived in yonder house." He pointed at an empty hut across the muddy expanse. Damaged by the storm, it looked fit to house hogs.

"You know the family's name?"

"Something like a bird name. Dove. No, no. Finch."

"Uh-uh," said the other in the mud. "Finchum. Not Finch."

"It was just Finch," the first said. "I swear."

"Finchum," said the rail-walker. "It was Finchum."

"Do any of you know where they went, or why?"

The girl said, "They were having no good fortune here. This mountain is mining out. It never was a really big strike to start with, and now it's busting. That's what my father says, anyway."

"So they moved on elsewhere. Any idea where?"

"I don't know about them in particular, but a lot of folks who left were headed for the high towns," said the eldest boy. "Just about everybody who leaves Millrace is going to the high towns, where there's silver."

"High towns?"

"Yeah. You know, the ones like Barrow, and Crowtown, and Marrowbone. They're all higher in the mountains than this one. They're up so high you got to boil your beans for hours just to cook 'em. That's what my pa says."

Penn stared at the mud below him, struggling not to look as disheartened as he felt. He'd really thought he'd find Nora here. "I reckon the high towns are where I'll have to look, then."

"How'd you lose your sister?"

Penn glanced at his questioner, the girl. He paused, then said, "I lost her in a way no one should ever have to lose a sister. I saw her given away to a man, like she was no more than a calf or a dog, when I was but a boy."

"Given away?" the girl repeated, looking perplexed.

"You know," the younger boy said. "She was a *slave*." He said the final word in the kind of whisper reserved for delicate subjects.

"Oh!" the girl said. She stared at Penn like he suddenly had become someone else.

"How long have these Finches, or Finchums, been gone?" he asked.

"I don't know. Two or three months."

"They must have left here before your marshal came into office. He knew of no Negro women in Millrace."

The elder boy gave Penn a very odd look. "Marshal? There ain't no marshal in Millrace. Never has been."

It took a moment for that to register. "Sure there is! His name's Jack Fifer. I met him coming down the mountain, him and his deputy, a black fellow like me, name of Bee."

"Jack Fifer? Never heard of him," the boy said. "I can tell you that, whoever he is, he ain't marshal here. Ain't no marshal here, like I said.

Ain't even no real town, nobody to even pay a marshal."

Penn paused. "And no jail?"

"No jail."

"How about a Methodist preacher . . . recently killed?"

"There's no Methodist preacher here. And nobody's been killed."

Penn was thoroughly disturbed at once. "Then I was lied to. And I turned a fellow over to a marshal who ain't really a marshal at all."

"What are you talking about?" the girl asked. Then, abruptly, she yelled, teetered, and fell off the rail on the outer side. She scratched the side of her head on a post on the way down.

The girl splattered in the mud, lay there a moment, then burst out wailing, holding her hand to her head. Penn rushed over to her and helped her to sit up.

"There, young lady, just rest easy. That's a hard spill you took there."

The girl cried out, "I'm cut!" The other two children looked on with great interest.

"Let me see," Penn said.

The girl lifted her hand. A small trickle of blood was running down her cheek from a cut near her temple. It was very minor, not likely to leave so much as a faint scar. Penn told her to hold his handkerchief tight to the wound.

A scar . . . McCutcheon . . .

Penn rose suddenly, eyes wide. "Dear Lord, I remember now!" he said.

The children looked at him in confusion.

He turned and hurriedly led his horse away without a word. He mounted and rode out of Millrace, heading back the way he'd come, as fast as he could go.

It all made sense now, and it scared him to death.

Johnny Bee, former slave, frequent drunkard, occasional strong-arm robber, and twice a killer whose crime went undetected, grunted and staggered back, his jaw throbbing. He stumbled to the ground, landing on his rump, and put a hand to his injured face.

He glanced up just in time to see the booted foot of the man he was fighting with come swinging at his head. Bee dodged to one side, shot a hand out to grab the other man's ankle, and sent his antagonist tumbling with a yank. Bee was up in a second, coming in on the other fighter with his knee in his belly. He swung three times, laying hard blows on alternating sides of his foe's face.

Standing back, Jack Fifer was very much enjoying this fight. Jim McCutcheon had come out of unconsciousness shortly after they'd reached this remote clearing, and when he'd realized he was back in the hands of the same men he'd narrowly escaped before the storm set in, he'd gotten violent very fast. Johnny Bee had been glad to oblige McCutcheon if it was a fight he wanted, especially since McCutcheon was weak, clumsy and dazed from his injuries, and had not a prayer of defeating the clear-headed Johnny Bee. Half the blows McCutcheon landed were by accident.

Fifer watched Bee pound the young man for a while, then intervened. "Hold up, Johnny! We don't want him knocked out again! We want him to be able to enjoy the full experience of what's coming to him."

Bee stopped his pounding long enough to spit into McCutcheon's face, then crawled off him, keeping a hand gripped tightly in McCutcheon's hair. He yanked hard.

"Get up, you!" Bee barked. "We got a hanging to attend to!"

McCutcheon struggled to his feet with difficulty, unable now to fight back.

"If you hang me . . ." he gasped, ". . . you're hanging an innocent man. I stole . . . none of them horses."

"You can tell it to the Almighty soon enough," Fifer said. Me and Johnny, we ain't interested."

Fifer had a rope in hand and was studying

the various trees around the clearing, looking for the best hanging limb. "There we go," he said, nodding. He already had the noose tied as he walked over and tossed it up, sending it smoothly arcing across the limb he'd selected. It swung ominously.

McCutcheon knew he had to make his break now or he would never find another chance. These men were serious about stringing him up, and all for something he'd not done.

Johnny Bee still had McCutcheon by the hair. McCutcheon swung his head hard, jerking free and wincing at the painful loss of some of his top thatch, and ran.

Bee was on him in a moment, driving him facedown to the ground, pulling his wrists around behind and clamping his arms against the small of his back.

"Give me something to tie up his hands with, Jack!" Bee said.

Fifer pulled out a knife and cut off a length of the trailing end of the hanging rope, a general-use lariat he always carried looped on his saddle. Bee had the young man's hands tightly bound within a minute.

"That'll hold him," he said. He dragged his victim to his feet again. "How you want to go about this, Jack? Put him on a horse and run it out from under him?"

"Naw. Keep it simple. Put the noose around his neck and we'll pull him up off the ground. Let him choke it out slow. That's the best a damned horse thief deserves."

Chapter Four

The young man struggled as best he could to keep them from getting the noose around his neck, but he was weakened, bound, and ultimately helpless. They got the loop around him within a couple of minutes and pulled it tight, the knot pressing behind his left ear.

"I didn't steal those horses," he said one last time. "I was hired to deliver them, I swear, and I didn't know they were yours."

"Sounds like good enough last words to me," Fifer said, and he and Bee heaved on the other end of the rope.

The rope jerked across the limb that held it. The noose constricted painfully around McCutcheon's neck, lifting him in the air. His toes struggled to maintain contact with the earth, but soon lost it.

Unable to breathe, his neck painfully stretching, throat pinching closed, McCutcheon hung between sky and earth, knowing that in minutes he would be dead. Because he hadn't fallen from a gallow's height his neck would be unbroken. There would be no swift and merciful death such as the one that came in a proper hanging, which snapped a man's neck and brought instant death. He would choke and suffer long before he died.

He saw them grinning, laughing, tying off the rope around a tree trunk. He kicked reflexively, but found that only made it worse—the noose tightened with each involuntary twitch. Panic and terror overwhelmed him, his instincts taking over, his body desperately fighting against the spectre of death.

His vision began to go black. He kicked some more, and his weight caused the straining rope to turn. He pivoted around to face the opposite direction, Bee and Fifer now unseen behind him.

In his fading field vision he saw a third man there, standing at the edge of the forest. A black man, with a rifle upraised and seemingly aimed squarely at the hanging man's face.

Shoot me, McCutcheon pleaded mentally, unable to speak. *Shoot me and let me die quickly, not like this!*

The rifle blasted. McCutcheon saw the flash of it just as his vision blacked out totally, hearing the gun's crack as if through great mounds of thick cotton.

*   *   *

Jack Fifer cursed as the rope was cut by the rifle's slug, just above the noose. McCutcheon fell to the ground like a sack of feed.

The black-skinned intruder, whom Fifer recognized as the very same man who had handed over McCutcheon to them, levered a new round into the chamber.

Bee had removed his gunbelt before the fight with McCutcheon. It lay on the ground five feet from him. He started for it.

"I wouldn't," the newcomer said. "I'd hate to have to kill a man, especially one of my own race."

Bee froze and glared at the rifleman.

Jack Fifer still wore his gunbelt; his right hand hovered near the grip of his pistol, fingers twitching.

"You, on the other hand, I'd gladly shoot," Jake Penn said to him. "I seen now that you bear some resemblance to a fellow I knew as a boy. He had quite a tendency to beat his slaves, including even the youngest ones. I'll just paste his face on yours and put a slug through your belly in half a moment, sir, and that's no lie. You take that gunbelt off slow, and toss it over to me."

Jack Fifer complied unhappily.

"Good. By the way, in case you forgot, the

name's Jake Penn. Don't ever forget it. For if ever you hear of me again, you'd best head to other parts. If I lay eyes on either of you past this day, no matter where or when or how, I'll see you dead."

Penn made Bee edge over to his own gunbelt and kick it over to him. Rifle still upraised, Penn secured the gunbelts and laid them behind him. He knelt and loosened the noose around McCutcheon's neck, using one hand. He felt around the base of the ear.

"He's still alive. Lucky for you, Mr. Fifer. I'd have been forced to execute you for murder if he'd been dead."

Fifer said, "What do you care about that horse thief? You said he tried to shoot you!"

"I'm a man with a problem, sir. My memory goes bad on me sometimes. Young McCutcheon there has been familiar to me from the moment I saw his face . . . but it wasn't until I got to Millrace that it all came back clear. It's a long story, nothing that concerns you. It comes down to the fact that me and that young man's family have some important history that we share, and I owe this fellow some protection. Now, you there, Mr. Bee. Tie your partner face-first to yonder tree."

"What?"

"Do it. And make the ropes tight enough to hurt. Anything less is too loose."

Within two minutes, Jack Fifer was hugging the tree, cheek against trunk, his wrists tightly bound around the far side.

Jake Penn, having removed the noose from the young man's neck, used it to tie Bee in that manner to another tree.

The two would-be killers of Jim McCutcheon were now helpless, effectively and ludicrously trapped with no hope of wriggling free.

Jake Penn stood back and smiled, admiring his work.

"You can't leave us here like this!" Fifer said. "We'll die! We'll be eat up by a bear!"

"Not likely. But if you are, you'll be no deader than you would have made my young friend here."

"Why do you call a man friend when you said yourself he tried to kill you?"

"As I said, there's history between me and this young man. But enough of that. I suggest that you gentlemen keep your throats cleared so you can holler loudly. You yell long enough, and somebody will come cut you free. But you wait a full hour before you send up the first shout. If you don't, I'll hear, and I swear I'll come back and shoot you both. You understand me?"

"You're a damned uppity nigger," Fifer said.

Johnny Bee flicked his eyes toward his partner, obviously offended to hear him speak so. But he said nothing.

"So I've been told more than once," Penn replied. "Gentlemen, good day to you."

Penn walked over to McCutcheon, who was beginning to regain awareness, trying to sit up and rubbing his badly abraded neck. It would bear the mark of the rope for many days to come.

"Come on, Mr. McCutcheon," Penn said. "I'll help you stand. You well enough to ride?"

It took three tries for the young man to get his voice back. It was scarcely a whisper. "Yes . . . I think so. How . . . do you know me?"

"Later, my friend, later. It's time for us to make some distance now."

They took the gunbelts, and McCutcheon rode Fifer's horse while Penn hitched Bee's horse to his own on a long line. They rode down the mountain, away from Millrace, pausing to take a final look back at the two men tied helplessly in the clearing. The pair looked absurd, standing there embracing trees like lovers. Penn laughed aloud, and even McCutcheon, battered up as he was, managed a smile.

They traveled for a long time, McCutcheon often on the verge of fainting. They rode a long distance before they heard the first faint cries for help from Bee and Fifer far behind them.

Penn chuckled. Obviously the pair hadn't worked themselves free yet, and the fact they'd waited this long to begin yelling for help showed they had taken his warning seriously.

McCutcheon murmured and almost fell from his saddle. Penn reached over to steady him, something he'd done often over the last hour.

"Hold on, Mr. McCutcheon. We'll be on more level ground soon and it'll be easier to ride. You're hurt, and you need rest. I'm going to find you some shelter."

They rode another hour. McCutcheon fell into a sort of stupor, not quite aware of his surroundings or of the passing of time, but keenly aware of pain. It ran all through him, but centered on his neck. He coughed a couple of times, and the mere spasm of his throat hurt so badly he almost passed out.

"Storm's building up again," Penn said. "Looks like it could be as bad as the first one. We need to find somewhere to lay up as soon as we can."

Thunder rumbled across the vast Colorado sky. McCutcheon wondered again who Jake Penn was, and how he knew him, but found that when he tried to speak, no sound would come.

The day rolled on, and by late afternoon the sky was rich with black clouds. Another round of stormy weather was coming fast. Penn had them halt. "Look there . . . see that cabin? Looks empty. I think we've found our shelter."

It was an old hunter's cabin, maybe once the refuge of some solitary mountain man. It was shabby, old, and would probably leak badly when the rain hit, but McCutcheon was happy to see it. Shelter represented safety, and a place to rest. He'd never felt such a need to collapse and sleep as he felt right now.

McCutcheon was not much aware of the next few hours. Penn made him a bed, using Jack Fifer's bedroll. McCutcheon slept for a while, and awakened to find the storm raging outside. Water dripped through the roof here and there, but not where he lay. He slept again.

Chapter Five

When McCutcheon opened his eyes next, the storm had slackened, and the cabin was filled with the aroma of cooking meat. He pushed himself up on his elbows and saw Penn kneeling beside a fire in an old and quite inefficient fireplace, frying rabbit meat in a pan.

Penn turned and grinned at him. "Hello, Mr. McCutcheon. Are you feeling better?"

McCutcheon tried to answer, but his voice was still a rasp.

"Hush, hush," Penn said. "That hanging put the squeeze on your talking box. You may not have a voice for a time. Are you hungry?"

McCutcheon nodded.

"Good. Because these vittles are ready now. You woke up at just the right time."

Penn served McCutcheon on a wooden trencher he'd found in the baggage of Fifer and Bee. McCutcheon ate and considered the fact that, if he hadn't been the horse thief Fifer and Bee had accused him of being, he certainly was now. And now only had they taken Bee and Fifer's horses with them, but also their saddlebags, bedrolls, and weapons.

Penn ate too, concentrating on his food and giving the younger man a chance to study him thoroughly.

McCutcheon took a long time to finish his meal, wincing with every swallow. When at last he'd laid his trencher aside, Penn looked at him. "I guess it's as good a time as any for us to have that talk about how it is that I know who you are, and why I've done what I have."

McCutcheon nodded.

"I'm Jake Penn, Mr. McCutcheon. And we met once before, years ago. You were but a child then, and I was a much younger man."

McCutcheon's puzzlement was plain on his face.

"Tell me: Is your father still living? And your mother?"

McCutcheon shook his head.

"I'm sorry to hear it. The colonel was a fine man, mighty good to me. And your mother as well. I'll always remember the gentleness she showed to a scared, fleeing slave trying to make his way to Canada."

McCutcheon's eyes revealed the dawning of understanding.

Penn produced a dry cigar, set it in his mouth, and lighted it before he went on. "It was 1859. Early spring. I was making my way up from Alabama through Tennessee, along the Underground Railroad. It brought me to your father's 'station.' He hid me; your mother fed me. And I remember their young son, how he fell down while he was showing me where I could hide beneath the floor of a woodshed. I remember how he cut himself pretty fierce along the side of the face, and how I pushed a cloth against it to try to stop the bleeding. And I remember telling that boy that the cut didn't look bad enough to scar." Penn smiled, lifted his finger, and traced a line along his own temple. "I reckon I was wrong."

"I remember," McCutcheon rasped.

Penn grew serious. "If I'd realized it was you, Mr. McCutcheon, I never would have turned you over to them two. From the moment I saw you, I knew there was something about your face, that scar in particular, that nagged at my mind. But I just couldn't make sense of it. Not until I saw a child in Millrace fall down and get a similar kind of cut to what you did . . . and then it all came rushing back, like a flood. I realized the mistake I'd made.

"I should have realized it sooner, when I first heard your name. I should have placed it right away, for I've striven never to forget the names of the people who helped me on my run to freedom.

"Colonel McCutcheon was a good man, a fine man, and I'm mighty sorry to hear he's gone. So though I can't do anything directly to thank him for what he done for me, I can sure tend to the welfare of his son."

McCutcheon shrugged and nodded, uncomfortable, not looking Penn in the eye. He wasn't a man at ease with heartfelt conversations.

Penn leaned closer. "I want to say something to you real sincerely, Mr. McCutcheon. I want you to know I'm mighty, mighty sorry I struck you so hard with that rifle back in the cave, though I hope you'll realize that I didn't know the full situation when I done it . . . and you *had* taken a shot at me, even though maybe you didn't really mean to. And I'm sorrier yet that I believed them two rogues were peace officers, and gave you over to them. I should have known such a tiny place as Millrace would have no hired law. I should have made sure of who and what they were before I let them have you. I'm only glad I was able to track them down and get there before they'd killed you."

McCutcheon gently rubbed his neck.

"Let me ask you something," Penn said, chewing on the cigar. "I been thinking. When you woke up in that cave and grabbed my rifle, you said something about not letting me hang you as a horse thief. I'm going to guess that you thought I was Johnny Bee. Am I right?"

McCutcheon nodded.

Penn reached over and gently patted McCutcheon's shoulder. "I'm glad neither of us succeeded in getting the other one killed. And I pledge to you right now that I'll stay with you until you're healed up. It's a way I can say I'm sorry, and a way I can thank your late father and mother for the kindness they showed a fleeing slave, despite all they had to lose by doing so. I'll never be able to do enough for you to really pay them back, Jim McCutcheon."

McCutcheon nodded, clearly ill-at-ease over all of this.

"You rest," Penn said. "When you get your voice back, we can talk some more."

Privately, though, he wondered if McCutcheon would get his voice back at all, or if the hanging rope had done injury that would never fully heal.

Chapter Six

Jake Penn knew it would be days before McCutcheon was sufficiently recovered from his ordeal to be able to travel. Though he was eager to get on to the higher mining towns and continue his search for his lost sister, he laid aside his plans for the moment in deference to taking care of his new companion.

Penn's fears for McCutcheon's voice appeared to be borne out during the first couple of days, during which there was no noticeable improvement. On the third day, though, McCutcheon was able to speak above a whisper, weakly in the morning, much louder by afternoon.

McCutcheon was obviously deeply relieved, and Penn was glad for him.

To keep them fed, Penn snared more rabbits, scoured the summer woods and meadows for natural edibles, and dipped into his own stock of trail food, and the smaller stock he found in

Fifer's packs. He was an able cook, and McCutcheon quickly came to appreciate the meals Penn served.

On the third night, Penn told McCutcheon his story. Leaning against the wall, he stared at the corner as he spoke.

"I was born in Alabama, grew up a slave, and saw my family hurt and mistreated, my father nothing but a mule for labor all his days. My mother and older sister, God rest their souls, were badly misused by the son of our master.

"I saw my younger sister, Nora, taken away from the family when she was no more than twelve years old to pay off a gambling debt. Given to, like she was no more than a saddle, or a rifle. I feared the use that probably was in mind for her, for she was a pretty girl.

"There were many other such things that happened through the years, things I see no need to tell tonight. But what I will say is that through all the evils I saw, through all the living as property instead of a human being, I gained an ache for freedom that burned through me, and kept me alive when I saw not much worth living for.

"I rebelled against being a slave, did everything I could to defy it. I taught myself to read and write. I learned every skill a man needed to know to live free on his own, which was my intention. Knowing I was bound for Canada someday, I even taught myself to speak some French, using a schoolbook I took . . . but I didn't steal it. No, sir. I never took nothing in my life that I didn't either have good moral grounds for taking or that I didn't pay for. It's the way I was taught, and the way I've tried to live."

"As a boy I listened to every whispered, secret story I could about the great Underground Railroad, on which a man could travel from 'station' to 'station,' and find his way to the free land in the high north. I longed to go, and would have gone long before I did if not for my parents getting old and needing my care. When their last days finally came, I was left alone.

"I fled two days after I buried my parents and headed north, following the way I'd been taught by those who knew of the Railroad. All along I found good people, better than I'd ever known, willing to take every kind of risk to help a man like me."

Penn reached up and swiped away a tear. He made no effort to hide it, which astounded McCutcheon, who'd hidden almost every emotion for years, fearing it would make him seem weak.

There was certainly nothing weak about Jake Penn, though. His honesty and sincerity were fiercely proud.

"I remember every face among them, and every name of any of them that allowed me to learn their names. Your father was one of them, Jim. He introduced himself and your mother . . . you were such a young boy at that time! Your family saved my life. I'd been nearly caught the day I reached your station. If not for the colonel intervening, putting off them who were after me, I'd never have made it past that night. I've have been captured, and worse.

"When I was finally safe past your family's station, I continued my journey. I reached the border and went into Canada, and there, for the first time in my life, I felt truly free. It was like the Promised Land.

"There I stayed, but then the war broke out back down in the States. When the Union commenced to forming regiments of black soldiers, I knew I had to go back. I did, and joined the U.S. Army. I did my job. I fought hard, and well.

"When the war was done, I didn't know what I'd do, so I did a little of everything. I roamed the country, working where I could. I saw the way my people suffered, saw them trying to make their way, learning how to live as free people. But you ain't free, not really, when everyone around you tries to find other ways to hold you down and keep you back. In some ways, times were worse for many Negro folks when their slavery was over. That was wrong. And it was a sad thing to see.

"I wondered many times about my sister Nora. Where was she? What had happened to her? Were times good or bad for her? I'd felt all along like I should have found her before I ran for Canada . . . I knew I couldn't really have done it, not with me on the run like I was. Yet I felt I should have tried.

"I wanted to look for her after the war, but I had to concern myself with trying to make a living. I worked in every sort of trade, all over the country. I'd keep my ears open, ask questions to see if I could find some clue about Nora . . . but I never found much. I tried my best to just forget about her.

"I ran across another man like myself one day, a former slave and a former soldier. We struck off well with one another and decided we'd just partner up and leave it all behind us for a time.

"We got ourselves some horses, some rifles, packsaddles, traps, and such, and crossed the Mississippi and just kept going. We didn't worry about what land we were on, or whose.

"We were skilled men, both of us; we knew how to live on the land, and off the land, without being seen, smelt, heard. We were like ghosts roaming around the country, going places most people will never go, seeing things most will never see. Happy times, those were. Very happy times indeed.

"I learned to survive during those years. I might have stayed in that life, always moving away from civilization, always living in the mountains and in the open country . . . but a man can't put all his past behind him. I began to dream about Nora, and fear for her. I would wake up in the night with the strongest notion that she was hurt, or sick, and calling for me. Just a silly thing, I guess, but it would sometimes overwhelm me so much I could hardly draw my breath.

"I told my partner about it, eventually. He told me it was because Nora was off somewhere in need of her brother. And it was my duty to find her.

"I knew he was right. I left him, and came back across the big river. I traveled to the places where Nora and I had been, asking questions, talking to kin and to folks who had known us. I even found family of the man who she'd been given to. I began to look for clues again, seeking any hint about what might have become of her. I've been searching for her ever since."

McCutcheon said, "How close have you come to actually finding her?"

"Close is a hard distance to measure, Jim. If

I'm trying to find you, and you're a thousand miles away, or even if you're just on the other side of the wall, what difference does it make if we never come together? I feel I've been near a time or two, but far away many more times than that. But I don't know. It's all just feelings anyway. I can't prove I've been close to her, if it's proof you're asking for. I can't say I *know* . . . I just *think*."

"Do you think you're near her now?"

"Maybe. Maybe. I'd been given strong indication I might find her in Millrace, yet I didn't. But I did speak to some children there, and they told me there'd been a Negro woman there, name of Nora, who had gone off to the higher mining towns. Barrow, Marrowbone, them towns. It could be that this Nora is my sister. Though I can tell you one fact I've learned solid over the past few years: there's more than one Negro woman named Nora in this nation. I think I've met half of them so far. Maybe the next one I meet will be the right one."

"So why are you here now? Why aren't you out trying to find her?" McCutcheon asked.

"Because I ain't going to let the one and only son of Colonel McCutcheon lie hurt and weak with no one to attend him."

"You needn't tend to me now. I'm stronger. I can talk again."

"You took a hard pounding. You'll take some time to heal."

"I'm a fast healer. You need to get on and find your sister."

"I'll get around to it soon enough."

"Ain't you in a hurry to find her?"

"I been in a hurry for years now. I can afford to wait a few days." Penn lifted one brow. "I'm beginning to think you're trying to get rid of me."

"I suppose I'm not used to being beholden to someone for my life. And you've saved my bacon twice."

"I'm going to stay until you're up to taking full care of yourself. Then I'll go."

"Aren't you afraid she might be getting off to somewhere else while you're sitting here?"

"Listen: I asked the good Lord to let me find Nora, if he'd allow it. And one night he whispered to me that he would. That means that there's a rendezvous set out there in the future somewhere, and neither me nor her will miss it. So I don't have to worry about things such as you said. It's meant to be, so it will be."

"That's a peculiar way to think, if you don't mind me saying so."

"Maybe so. But it's my only way."

There was a lapse in the conversation. Penn broke it after a few moment.

"I've told you my story. I'd like to hear yours, if you'd be willing."

McCutcheon seemed to stiffen. "I don't have a story to tell you."

"Every man has a life. So every man has him a story to tell."

"My story's not worth hearing."

"Tell me, at least, how you came to leave Tennessee and come West."

"I left after my parents died."

"No inherited house and lands to keep you home?"

"There was an inheritance, yes. And I've said all I want to say about it. Not trying to be rude. But I really don't want to say no more."

After that, Penn did not ask again.

Chapter Seven

The truth was that Penn required no more information to figure out, in broad terms, what had happened to Jim McCutcheon.

Penn supposed that Jim McCutcheon had followed the well-trodden trail of the proverbial prodigal son. He'd cashed in his inheritance, taken it West, and lost it. Probably gambling, maybe women, maybe bad investments or simply incompetent handling. Maybe it was stolen from him. Whatever had happened, he surely wasn't a monied fellow now. McCutcheon had abject poverty written in his very look and manner.

McCutcheon remained steadfastly unwilling to talk about his story, but in a later conversation he did explain to Penn his troubles with Bee and Fifer.

He'd been duped, McCutcheon said, by a man who had hired him to herd horses to a buyer in

Millrace. All the paperwork was there: a bill of sale, a letter of permission. In dire need of work, McCutcheon had taken on the job, only to be intercepted along the way by Bee and Fifer. They declared themselves the true owners of the horses, and provided convincing evidence to back up the claim. It was obvious that the horses, which they'd been tracking, had been stolen from them, and the papers McCutcheon carried were forgeries.

McCutcheon, who had no impulse to argue over the matter, turned the horses over to them, abandoning his mission to deliver them. But he found this did not satisfy the pair. Bee and Fifer were determined to see someone punished for the theft of their horses, and Jim McCutcheon had seemed the obvious choice. They'd caught him, and prepared to hang him, but he escaped and hid in an empty cabin, the same one that Penn had seen washing over the falls in the storm. The horses, ironically, had been scattered and lost, terrified by the fierce storm.

The story beyond that, Penn already knew.

When McCutcheon was through, Penn asked him: "Tell me, Jim—do you always find this kind of trouble for yourself wherever you go?"

McCutcheon replied, "No. A lot of times I find much worse."

Penn laughed, but noticed that McCutcheon didn't even crack a smile.

When McCutcheon was well again and the time of parting came, the moment proved to be unexpectedly clumsy for both him and Penn.

Outside the little cabin, astride Fifer's horse, McCutcheon looked at Penn, smiled tightly, and thrust out his hand. "Many thanks to you," he said. "I hope you find your sister soon. I think it's a fine thing, you looking for her."

"Thank you. Best to you in all you do."

"Where exactly will you go now, Penn? The high mining towns?"

"Yes. Maybe I'll find her there."

"Well if I should run across her myself, I'll tell her you're looking for her," Penn said.

"I'm obliged. Where are you bound?"

"I don't know. Maybe Denver. It don't matter much where you are when you're me."

"I'd surely like to know more about you, Jim. I suspect you're an interesting young man."

"Just a young man whose luck is always the bad kind. That's all."

"Well, maybe that will change. Beautiful town, Denver. It would be a good place for a man to settle down and make a home. You might find better times there."

"Maybe. What's home for you, Penn?"

"Wherever I am at any given moment."

"Then we're alike in that way, me and you."

They shook hands again, and rode off in different directions, neither with any reason to believe that, beyond the unforseeable connivances of the same chance that had brought them together at the waterfall, they ever would meet again.

Jim McCutcheon rode slowly through the outskirts of Denver, heading deeper into town. He found little to dislike as he looked around.

This was a busy city, the kind of place around which the promise of a bright future hung like a golden veil. Though weary from the trail, McCutcheon was invigorated merely by riding through the streets.

It was good to be back among real people once again, civilized people. He'd been in the mining camps too long.

Yet Denver posed a challenge. He'd have to find a way to make a living here during the time he chose to remain. It wouldn't be long— McCutcheon never stayed anywhere long—but a man had to eat even in the short term. By now, though, he was virtually penniless, his supply of food almost exhausted.

He rode through the brightest and most affluent streets, fantasizing about how fine it would be to be able to make his life in these environs. Ah, yes, he belonged here! But then, with a sigh, he turned his mount down a side street to go in search of the seamier part of town. Every city had one, and it was in Denver's, he knew, that he would be most likely to find ready work.

A woman came out of a nearby shop. When she closed the door behind her, the sound caught his ear and made him look her way. She was a pretty woman, young, and their eyes met and held. He smiled and touched his hat; she smiled back. But he saw her eyes drop slightly, and knew she was studying his neck, which still bore the burn of the rope with which he'd been hanged.

He became self-conscious, embarrassed. He wanted to assure this unknown woman that she didn't understand, that despite whatever she was thinking, he wasn't some criminal who'd managed to cheat the gallows, nor some would-be suicide who'd turned coward and saved himself at the last moment.

By now, though, she was past him, hurrying on down the boardwalk. He turned and went on his way, cursing the mark on his neck. It did seem to be fading, but not quickly enough to suit him.

What if a trace of it always remained? He'd

go through life with people whispering and wondering, and closing doors before he could reach them. He tugged at his coat collar, turning it up, trying to hide the rope burn.

He found the narrowest, most dilapidated street of them all and rode slowly down it, dead-center, looking at the low-roofed buildings on all sides. Most were saloons, others gambling halls or dance parlors, and some businesses that bore no labels but whose function was made obvious by the dark-eyed women who peered out of windows and doorways, trying to look enticing but mostly looking sad and worn.

At last McCutcheon stopped his horse in front of a saloon that, for some intuitive reason, struck him as promising. He tied off at a hitching post and headed for the door, above which swung a sign saying DRAKE'S BEVERAGES.

The proprietor was a beefy man with the odd name of Curtsy Drake. McCutcheon fought back a smile when he heard it.

"Work?" Drake asked when McCutcheon had explained why he'd come. "What kind of work?"

"Whatever you have. I can do most anything."

"You can tend bar?"

"I can." McCutcheon, in fact, had never tended a bar in his life, but surely it wasn't that hard.

Drake looked him over, evaluating. "You ain't the biggest fellow on the block. Can you fight?"

McCutcheon assumed he was talking about fisticuffs for entertainment and competition. Some of the rougher saloons had fighting men who'd take on all comers out back of the place, for a cut of the wagered money. "I don't know that fighting is really what I had in mind," said McCutcheon.

"Then I can't use you." Drake turned away.

McCutcheon was surprised by the brusqueness of this brush-off. "Listen, I'll sweep up, tend the bar, deal with the rowdy drunks—"

"You told me you can't fight."

"I don't fight for money. But I can deal with drunks, if that's what you were talking about."

"What about cleaning spittoons?"

McCutcheon paused, then said, "If that's what's needed."

"Clean the outhouse pit when it needs it?"

The pause was a little longer. McCutcheon hoped not to be around in this job long enough for that duty to fall to him. He wanted only a few dollars to pocket before drifting on to the next place. He decided to take his chances that privy-cleaning time wouldn't roll around during his tenure.

"I'll do whatever's needed. I'm a hard worker, Mr. Drake."

Drake thought about it, then talked to McCutcheon a little more. But when McCutcheon left, he did so still unemployed.

He'd noticed that Drake had stared at his rope-burned neck. No wonder he hadn't wanted to hire him.

He spent the rest of the day visiting other saloons, and having the same bad luck at each one.

Discouraged, McCutcheon went looking for a woodshed in which to sleep at the end of the day. But he worried about feeding his horse. He'd bought oats on his way in to Denver, but that supply was now gone.

Even getting a job wouldn't help in that regard, because pay day would surely be a week away, and his horse needed oats right now.

There was only one thing to do. McCutcheon found an empty shed big enough for both him and his horse, and stabled the horse there. Then, as darkness fell, he took an empty bucket and left his new home.

He'd seen a livery stable on a nearby street earlier in the day, over near Drake's saloon. Keeping to the alleys and circling around the backs of buildings, he headed in that direction.

Chapter Eight

Jim McCutcheon was not a thief by nature, and though breaking into the livery was ludicrously easy and the place was utterly unguarded, it took him a few moments to actually work up the will to dip his bucket into the bin of oats.

As he did it, he thought of Jake Penn and his story of teaching himself a bit of French using an old schoolbook. Penn stressed that he'd paid for the book.

McCutcheon wondered if it was true. Why would a man who was born into slavery feel the slightest sense of obligation to pay back the same system that had enslaved him, especially for something so insignificant as a used book? McCutcheon doubted he'd have been so honorable in that situation.

Whoever and whatever Jake Penn was, McCutcheon thought, he must be a better man than most. The kind of man you admired and resented at the same time.

He fed his horse the stolen oats and told himself he was only doing what he had to do. Yet he felt awfully guilty.

Jake Penn, paying for that blasted French book. Jake Penn risking his life to rescue a fellow who had shot at him. Jake Penn putting aside his quest for his sister just to take care of someone for the sake of something that had happened seventeen years ago. Jake Penn, returning to the United States to fight in a war he could have avoided, just because he believed he should. Jake Penn, searching for a long-missing sister he couldn't even prove was alive . . . all because he believed he should.

What was Jake Penn, anyway? Some kind of saint? Who was he to go around making Jim McCutcheon feel morally inferior?

"I can't help all that's happened to me, you know," McCutcheon said to his horse. "It wasn't my fault I lost my inheritance . . . not entirely my fault, anyway. And it wasn't my fault that I got thrown into this life. I'd do better if I could. Bad luck, that's all it is. A man can't help his luck, can he?"

The horse merely looked back at him.

"Don't look at me that way!" McCutcheon said. "That's all I could get for you. And if you're hungry, then I'm hungrier. If I don't find work soon, I'll be stealing food for myself the next time."

McCutcheon was back at Curtsy Drake's the next afternoon, weak with hunger. It was the time of day that Drake usually showed up at the place, which operated from noon until two o'clock in the morning every day.

Drake glowered at McCutcheon. "Don't I know you?"

"I was in here yesterday," McCutcheon said. "Asking for work."

"Oh, yeah. Yeah."

"Now I'm back . . . asking again."

"Why do you think I'd need you now when I didn't need you yesterday?"

"Listen, sir, I'll admit that I'm desperate. I'm about out of money. I had no supper last night. I even had to steal oats from that livery yonder just to feed my horse. I—"

"You stole oats from where?"

Blast it! Why had he let that slip out? There was no backing away now. "Uh . . . that livery over there."

"That's *my* livery!"

"What?"

"I own that stable! It was me you stole those oats from!"

McCutcheon didn't know what to say.

"Hell, young fellow, I guess you *will* be working for me now!"

"Beg your pardon?"

"How much did you take? You either pay for it, or you work it off. You understand me?"

"Well . . . yes. Of course."

"You got no money, right?"

"No sir. I'm cleaned out."

"Then you can start by sweeping that floor. Get rid of all that old sawdust. And bring in fresh sawdust from the shed in the back."

"Yes, sir."

"Get to it. Now."

"Yes, sir. Right away."

He couldn't say why, but McCutcheon had a good feeling about this turn of circumstances. As soon as he finished sweeping out the saloon, and spread fresh, sweet-smelling sawdust across the floor, he had a sense that luck was going his way.

He'd even been able to sneak a couple of crackers from behind the bar. It took the edge off his hunger and gave him a bit of energy.

He finished his job, and headed behind the bar. He found a clean rag and some dirty glasses, and began swiping them out. He stacked the glasses neatly in two pyramids, then cleaned the big, cracked mirror that hung behind the bar.

And so it went, him continuing to labor, asking no direction or permission, and avoiding Drake, who remained busy and distracted, hardly aware of McCutcheon at all.

Midnight came and went; McCutcheon was still there. An increasingly rough and rowdy element began to trickle in. One man, a wiry but belligerent loudmouth who was drunk even before he entered the door, tried his best to stir up trouble.

McCutcheon saw his opportunity. Before Drake could reach the man to deal with him, McCutcheon stepped forward and confronted the man.

"Get out," McCutcheon said firmly, his flinty gaze locking with the drunk's bleary eyes.

The man gaped at McCutcheon, then laughed. "Look there!" he said, pointing at McCutcheon's neck. "Look at that rope ring around there! Somebody try to hang you, boy? Or did you do it yourself?"

McCutcheon pointed at the door. "There's the way out. Use it."

"Tried to hang hisself, then lost the nerve!" the drunkard chortled. "What was it, boy, some woman? That why you done it?"

Drake came to McCutcheon's side, and McCutcheon had the strongest feeling that the saloon owner had only just now noticed that the young man he'd brought in to work off one bucket's worth of stolen feed oats was still around and working.

"I can take care of this, Mr. Drake," McCutcheon said.

"No reason you should have to."

"Let me. I want to show you I can handle myself. I can do good work for you."

The drunk pulled out a knife. "I'll cut your head off and use that rope burn for a guide!"

Drake cast a glance at McCutcheon. "You still want to deal with him?"

McCutcheon eyed the knife, but said with bravado, "I've handled worse."

The drunk lunged at him, blade-first. He didn't feint—he intended to cut and cut deep.

McCutcheon grabbed the man's wrist, twisted it hard, and made him drop the knife. Luckily, the fellow was small, and it wasn't hard to turn his arm behind his back and secure a strong grip around his neck. McCutcheon waltzed him to the door and shoved him out, then went back, picked up the knife, and tossed it out after him.

"We're glad to have your business, my friend, but you understand we can't have you trying to pick fights and cut folks," he called out, doing his best to sound like a man who was calmly in charge of the situation, even after almost taking a blade in his flesh.

The man outside cursed and threatened, but he was already going on his way. McCutcheon turned to Drake.

"I believe he'll be no further trouble," he said, smiling. "Am I hired?"

Drake frowned. "Just how *did* you get that rope mark there?"

"I'll tell you all about it . . . if you'll hire me. Please, sir. I've worked all evening just to show you I can."

"You ain't wanted by the law, are you?"

"No, sir."

Drake paused, sighed, then nodded. "What the devil. Young man, I reckon you just earned yourself a job."

Chapter Nine

Three nights later, after the place had closed, Drake poured McCutcheon a beer and had him sit down at a table.

McCutcheon saw a firing on the way, but Drake merely sat down across from him and said, "I want you to tell me how you came to have that rope scar."

Drake's voice was somewhat slurred. He'd begun drinking earlier in the evening while he tended the bar, and was well on his way to being thoroughly soused.

McCutcheon saw no reason to lie to his employer, so he told him the entire story, from his ill-fated effort to herd the horses that wound up stolen, on through his rescue from the noose by Jake Penn. He must have done a good job of it, because Drake listened, wide-eyed and fascinated.

But McCutcheon did not reveal one thing: his family's connection to the Underground Railroad. That remained a subject capable of stirring strong feelings, and experience had taught McCutcheon simply not to bring it up. He had no idea where Drake stood on such a controversial issue.

Drake, who was growing more mellow with every sip of liquor, obviously found Penn an interesting character and had many questions about him, most of which McCutcheon couldn't answer.

"Whoever he is, this Jake Penn must be some remarkable kind of darky," he said. "Standing up to a white man like that! Takes courage."

"Courage is something he seems to have in good supply," McCutcheon replied.

"Think of that . . . a man grows up a slave, flees to his freedom, then comes back to search for the sister he ain't seen since her girlhood . . . what a story!"

"His sister's name is Nora," McCutcheon volunteered, taking a sip from his glass. "Jake Penn hasn't seen her since she was a girl, but he seems sure he'll know her when he finds her."

"Sounds like wishful thinking," Drake said. "She got a last name?"

"Penn, I suppose, unless she's married, of course. I suppose her last name could be anything."

"Penn's got cussed little chance of finding

her," Drake said. "Sad to think about: roaming the country, looking for a woman he'll never find, always hoping for something that can't be. A true tragedy. Old Willie Shakespeare could have writ about this!"

McCutcheon was surprised that Drake even knew who Shakespeare was.

"Maybe he will find her," McCutcheon said. "He's determined, and he believes he's already come close a time or two. He also says he believes God has promised him he'll let him find her."

"He's a religious darky, then."

"I suppose. But he can handle himself as slick as the devil."

Drake leaned forward and examined McCutcheon's neck by the light of the table lamp. "I believe that mark's fading."

"I hope so. It gives people the wrong notions about me. I passed a woman on the street who all but ran from me when she saw it."

Drake drank in silence awhile longer, then leaned back in his chair. "You know, McCutcheon, I have a feeling about you. I see you as the kind who, given the right opportunity, could make a good life for himself."

McCutcheon laughed without mirth.

"What? That's funny?"

"You'd think it was funny, too, if you knew

all the things that have happened to me. I had that 'right opportunity' you talked about. And I lost everything."

"What do you mean?" Drake asked.

"I had an inheritance from my parents. A good one. I could have stayed where I was, kept the old home, invested the money as I'd been advised to do . . . but I was too stubborn. Too restless. I sold everything I had. Turned my inheritance into cash and headed west, thinking I'd become the biggest, most successful cattleman, or a merchant, or even the best horse trader that this country had seen. I had no specific plan beyond getting rich."

"And it didn't turn out so well, did it?"

"I made mistakes. Big ones. I invested half the money with men who turned out to be swindlers. The other half I thought I could use to make back the half I'd lost."

"How so? Better investment?"

McCutcheon took a swig and shook his head. He was honestly embarrassed to reveal the truth. "Cards."

"Oh. Lost it all, huh?"

"Lost it all."

"And now you're down to sweeping saloons and tossing out drunkards in a Colorado backstreet saloon."

McCutcheon raised his glass. "Here's to my new life."

"I'm more inclined to drink to forgetting the past and looking for new opportunities," Drake said.

McCutcheon laughed again. "There's no opportunities for Jim McCutcheon. I had my chance and lost it."

"*Pshaw!* The West is full of opportunities! This nation is growing. Why, in a matter of weeks, this territory we sit in will be a new state! You can start over, my friend. You can make something good of yourself. Look at me! When I came to Denver, I had nothing, not a cent. I worked as a teamster, then as a carpenter, then as a sign painter. All the while I saved my dollars, then found me a saloon keeper eager to sell and move away for reasons of his failing health. We struck a bargain, and here I am today. A successful saloon keeper! That, I'll drink to!"

With a big, bleary-eyed smile, Drake raised his glass then downed its contents with a big swallow.

McCutcheon looked around at the squallid saloon. If this was Drake's idea of success, then he and the man lived in two different conceptual worlds. McCutcheon had come west with a vision of sprawling lands, a fine house on a big spread of property, barns and cattle around, and a beautiful wife at his side, living like a baron and a king. It was a mocking vision now.

All that was left of his dream was bitterness, but it was a bitterness he clung to possessively, almost lovingly. McCutcheon was a young man furious at a world that had denied him all he wanted. He was not about to let it also deny him the pleasure of self-pity.

He and Drake finished their drinks, then had several others. Almost as an afterthought, Drake went to the cash box and removed money, which he handed to McCutcheon. "Your first pay," he said, "plus a bonus for having provided me good conversation this evening."

McCutcheon was pleased by the amount. He suspected he'd not have done nearly so well if Drake hadn't been in his cups. "Thank you," he said, pocketing the money before Drake had time to reconsider.

"You're quite welcome. Now, be off with you to your room. Where do you stay, come to think of it? Where could I find you if I needed you?"

"I've got a little place a couple of streets down," he said. "Temporary. I'll let you know when I get settled in more permanently."

"Good evening to you, Jim," Drake said. "I've enjoyed talking to you."

McCutcheon suspected he'd not find Drake so

jovial when the alcohol wore off. He hoped the barkeep wouldn't demand that bonus be returned.

"Good night, Mr. Drake."

McCutcheon walked out of the saloon and onto the dark and empty street. He strode along for a block or so, then cut right into an alley, heading for the woodshed that was his home. Not much of a place, to be sure, but it kept the weather out and cost nothing.

His route took him to a backstreet, really just a broad alleyway running a crooked route behind false-fronted commercial buildings. On the far side of the alleyway were huts and hovels of the poorest citizens, their windows dark at this hour, the occupants sleeping and dreaming dreams that McCutcheon could only suppose were as resentful and bitter as his own.

In only one window a light burned. Its glow was soft, diffused by the dirty sheet that hung inside the window as a curtain. McCutcheon passed that window along his way, and heard voices shouting from inside.

A man and a woman cursed one another. He tried not to listen.

He was almost past the little house when he heard the sharp slap of hand against flesh, and a simultaneous screech from the woman.

He winced and stopped. Some impulse told

him to go back and intervene. He heard more
slaps, then muffled screams.

Go back! that inner voice said. *Go back and
knock on the door. That's all it will take to stop it.
Just a knock.*

He didn't want to. It wasn't his affair. And
maybe what was going on in there wasn't as
bad as it sounded.

The man's voice grew louder, cursing the wailing and crying woman.

Why don't the neighbors wake up? McCutcheon
thought. *Why doesn't one of them do something?*

The voice inside replied: *Why don't* you *do
something?*

The beating went on still, but the woman
wasn't crying out so loudly now.

McCutcheon's next thought surprised him: *If
Jake Penn was here, he'd do something. When he
needs to, he gets involved.*

McCutcheon steeled his will. He *would* intervene, just like Penn had intervened to save him
from a lynching.

He strode back toward the hut, but noticed
that the inside of the dwelling had grown silent.

McCutcheon stood unmoving a moment, un-
sure what to do. Finally he turned and walked
away, heading again for his own rude quarters.

Whatever had gone on in there was finished
now. There was nothing for him to do.

He reached his woodshed, crawled onto the bed he'd improvised from some old blankets he'd found, and tried to sleep. But he couldn't. The screams of the unseen woman in that hut kept echoing through his head.

Chapter Ten

McCutcheon had trained himself to survive on little food and often had to go for remarkably long times indifferent to hunger. But when he awoke the next morning, he was unusually ravenous. His last meal had been early the evening before—crackers and pickled eggs in the saloon—and it hadn't held for long.

There was the further fact he had money in his pocket. Though McCutcheon planned to conserve his earnings as much as possible, he decided it surely wouldn't be extravagant, under the circumstances, to treat himself to a real cooked breakfast.

He left the woodshed on the sneak, barely getting away before hearing someone exit the nearby house, probably to gather firewood to cook a bit of breakfast. He headed down the alley and was well out of sight by the time he heard the woodshed door creak open. He hoped he'd hidden his blankets well enough. Some folks didn't take well to strangers turning their sheds into free hotels.

At least he didn't have to deal with his horse anymore. Drake was allowing him to stable it in his barn, taking a small cut out of McCutcheon's pay to cover the cost of the feed. But Drake had more than given that back the night before in the form of the bonus.

McCutcheon initially took the same route back the way he had come the prior night, then changed his mind when he remembered those screams emanating from that little hut. He didn't want to encounter that kind of awkward situation again. Taking a different route, he walked to a main street and found a café, where he ordered a large breakfast that he thoroughly enjoyed. He lingered over coffee, feeling grateful his work didn't begin until the afternoon.

When the lazy morning had passed and McCutcheon showed up at the saloon, he found Drake there early, looking irritable, probably hungover from the prior night's drinking. McCutcheon doubted he'd find an abundance of good humor in his employer this night, and worried again over the bonus he'd been paid.

Drake was engaged in conversation with a Denver policeman who had the loose collar and relaxed manner of an officer going off duty.

Drake hardly acknowledged McCutcheon's presence, being engrossed in what the policeman was telling him. McCutcheon could easily hear it all, and quickly began paying attention when he realized the situation being discussed.

". . . and when we brought him out, his nose was nearly flat against his face. She'd walloped him right across it with an iron skillet. Knocked him out cold as winter. But from the looks of things, she may have saved her life by doing it. He'd beaten on her awfully badly. He'd not have stopped until she was dead, as drunk as he was, if she hadn't stopped him first."

McCutcheon lingered near the bar, staying close enough to listen in, realizing this tale probably related to the unpleasantness he'd heard emanating from that little shack last night.

"What was it?" Drake asked, his voice whispery because it hurt for him to talk any louder. "Lovers' spat between husband and wife?"

"Love has very little to do with what goes on in that alley and that house," the policeman said. "The man puts out his own wife for prostitution. Can you imagine such a thing? But it's true. We'll catch him at it soon enough, and lock his sorry hind end up where it belongs. And if there's enough old unreconstructed Confederates around, they might even string up the sorry devil."

"Maybe she didn't want to live that kind of life anymore, and that's what they fought over," Drake speculated.

"Maybe. Whatever the case, if she hadn't got hold of that skillet, none of it would matter now. He'd have killed her, no question of it in my mind."

"How'd you hear about the fighting?"

"A neighbor sent out a boy to find a policeman so he could complain about the noise. What do you think of that? A woman's nearly beat to death, and all the neighbor is worried about is that she's squalling too loud to let him sleep. This old world is getting sorrier by the day, I'm here to tell you. People don't care anymore. A man in my job sees it all the time."

McCutcheon, guilt-stricken by the cop's last few comments, couldn't resist interrupting. "Pardon me, but could you tell me where this thing you're talking about happened?"

"Who's this?" the policeman asked Drake. Like most of his kind, he had learned to be suspicious of strangers, especially nosy ones.

"Newcomer to town. He works for me. You can talk in front of him."

"It happened in Reed Alley."

"Is that the one about a block from here, behind the row of buildings yonder way?"

"That's it. Tell me, son, why are you interested in this matter?"

McCutcheon wasn't inclined to answer that one fully. "I, uh . . . went home in that direction last night, and saw a policeman heading into that alley. That's all. I was just curious about what was going on. Maybe it was you I saw." He grinned.

"Maybe it was." The policeman had spotted the fading rope scar on McCutcheon's neck, and was studying it with a frown. "You wouldn't happen to know anything about that incident, would you?"

"No, sir, Mister . . ."

"Clair. Mortimer Clair."

"Did I hear you say a man was hit in the face with a skillet?"

"That's right. A black fellow," Clair said. "He's been patched up and she's locked up in the jail for the day, as much to calm her down as anything. And to let that husband of hers cool off a little so maybe he won't kill her when they're back together again."

"Skillet, huh?"

"Right across the face."

McCutcheon whistled softly, and made a painful face.

"I feel like I've been hit by a skillet myself," Drake said, rubbing his temples.

"You put some liquor away last night, did you, Curtsy?" the policeman asked.

Drake grunted and meandered away. McCutcheon busied himself cleaning glasses. Clair hooked a dried biscuit out of the biscuit bin and began to nibble on it.

"Tell me something, son. How'd you get that rope mark on your neck?"

It's a long story."

"I'm finished with my duty for today. I got time."

"I was accused of being a horse thief, though I wasn't. Two fellows strung me up, and a third got me down before it killed me. It wasn't a legal hanging. It was attempted murder."

The policeman swallowed a piece of the dry biscuit with effort. "I thought you said it was a long story."

"I gave you the short version."

"New in town, are you?"

"Yes, sir."

"Watch your step. You hear?"

"I always do."

McCutcheon was relieved to hear no one had been killed in that domestic brawl he'd overheard. But he also felt all the worse about having hesitated to intervene. He'd stood out there hanging fire in the alley while a woman was being beaten, a woman who'd saved herself not with any help from him, but by making a weapon out of the nearest kitchen utensil.

The matter remained on McCutcheon's mind the rest of the night. When he walked home, he took a different route than he had the night before, to be sure to avoid that little row of huts. He wasn't ready for any further moral testing.

He now lay on his blankets, mind turning.

What if Jake Penn had hesitated to come back and help me? What if I'd twisted on that rope only half a minute more? I'd be dead.

He vowed that next time he was faced with a chance to help out someone in need or danger, he'd do better. And he wouldn't hesitate. He'd do it readily, just like Jake Penn would.

Chapter Eleven

"Jimbo! What's the matter with you? You asleep on your feet?"

McCutcheon started, then looked around as if he had, indeed, just woken up. He was in the midst of the saloon, leaning on his broom, having been lost in a reverie after overhearing a comment that reminded him of a pleasant childhood experience. He'd been mentally reliving it, deep in thought for the past five minutes.

"What's wrong with you, son?" Drake said. His voice startled McCutcheon. "Are you going deaf on me? I need you to empty those spittoons there. And waste no time about it."

McCutcheon nodded, though his heart sank. A gruesome job, but it was necessary. Nothing was worse than leaving a full one around to get kicked over and spilled. Even the sawdust on the floor couldn't properly absorb a full spittoon, once spilled. McCutcheon had seen it happen once already in his brief employment here.

He carefully picked up the nearest spittoon. It sloshed with reeking brown spittle, and McCutcheon made a face as he carried it ahead of him, at arm's length.

He exited the back of the saloon, headed to the fence, and poured the foul matter over, glad for the fence because it stood between him and the splattering mess.

"What the hell!"

A man's voice yelled loudly from the other side of the fence. McCutcheon yanked the now-empty spittoon back across the fence and peered over the top, horrified to think he might have dumped that hideous slop onto someone.

In the darkness he saw the form of a man, standing there looking disheveled, his shirttail out, his pants held up around his waist by one hand. Beside him was an equally disheveled black woman, still in the act of quickly slipping her dress back on.

It wasn't hard for McCutcheon to guess what kind of woman she was, or the nature of the transaction he'd just interrupted.

"You almost got that mess all over me!" the man shouted. "I nearly got hit by them big splatters! Damn it all!"

"I'm sorry," McCutcheon said. "I didn't know anyone was back there."

"You should have looked."

"You're right. I should have—even though that's Mr. Drake's property back there, and not open to trespassing. Even so, I am awfully sorry."

"I got some of it on my dress," the woman complained. "It stinks!"

McCutcheon looked at her, and saw that she was bruised and battered, her lip swollen and a long, deep scratch down the side of her face.

At once McCutcheon's natural tendency to back away from the business of others asserted itself . . . but then he remembered Jake Penn.

"Has this man been beating you?" McCutcheon asked.

"That's a damned impudent question, you upstart!" the man protested.

"I didn't ask you. I asked her."

"He ain't been beating me," the woman said. "Somebody else done this. But I do thank you, sir, for you asking."

McCutcheon got the impression that she meant it. Probably few people ever showed much concern for her welfare, considering her line of work, and the color of her skin in a world where white men ruled supreme.

"I ought to come across that fence and make you lick out that spittoon!" the man seethed.

McCutcheon's temper flared. "Come on, then. You think you can do it, then come try! No, wait. Let me just come over there to you."

The man backed away. "Hold on, now. Hold on." He forced a laugh. "I was just joking with you, friend. No cause for us to have no more trouble, I don't reckon."

"I reckon not," McCutcheon said. "So maybe you ought to be a little slower to make threats. Now, you two best get along. You're on property belonging to Mr. Drake, and I don't think he'd like to know that there was such kind of things as what you were doing going on in his own back door."

"Come on," the man said to the woman, putting on his hat. "We'll find us a better place than this, Nora."

They strode away, and McCutcheon went back into the saloon. He put the emptied spittoon back in place and picked up another full one, then carried it back out the door and emptied over the fence like he had the first one.

He was turning to go back inside when it struck him.

Nora?

That's what the man had called her. She was a black woman, not old but no longer young either, and her name was Nora.

McCutcheon dropped the spittoon and vaulted

over the fence, barely clearing the slimy puddle of spittoon slop that he'd created. He dashed out through the lot between two buildings and onto the street, where he stopped and looked in both directions, hoping to spot them.

The street was empty. Nora and her customer had already found themselves some other secluded place.

McCutcheon stood there and caught his breath. He looked around one more time, then returned to the saloon.

Mortimer Clair had been a member of Denver's police force for almost exactly five years, and in that time he had gone from a clumsy neophite to a rather suave peace officer. He prided himself on never becoming disconcerted and losing his calm demeanor before the public eye.

Thus he was unpleasantly surprised when a hand touched his elbow as he stood leaning against a porch rail and caused him to start, lose his balance, and almost pitch over the rail. He yelled, and righted himself with a great flailing motion that lent him all the dignity of a flopping fish, receiving a giggle from some attractive young women passing by.

Clair turned on his heel to face whatever scoundrel had so made him embarrass himself.

He found himself face to face with the young man who worked for his friend, Curtsy Drake.

"Ah, it's you—our young hangman!" Clair said, letting his eye fall to the faint reddish mark that encircled the young man's neck. "What do you mean, coming upon me to startle me that way!"

"It wasn't intentional," McCutcheon said. "My name's McCutcheon, in case you've forgotten. I work over in Curtsy Drake's—"

"Yes, yes, I know who you are. Is there something I can do for you?"

"I think so. I saw you standing here, and it made me think of a question I need answered. The woman who was beaten in Reed Alley . . . what was her name?"

"Why are you so interested in that case? It's merely a Negro beating his wife. It happens all the time."

"I have personal reasons for wanting to know. If you would, can you tell me her name?"

"Well, I don't know I recall . . . wait." Clair pulled out a leather-bound note pad and made a show of flipping through it, his expression clearly designed to convey to McCutcheon that this was all indeed a great bother.

"Ah, yes. Here it is. Her name is Nora. Nora Jackson."

McCutcheon nodded. "I thought it might be. Thank you, Mr. Clair."

"You're welcome. And don't go sneaking up on me like that again, hear?"

McCutcheon walked slowly along the boardwalk, letting the afternoon sun bake his shoulders.

It hadn't been hard to piece together that the woman who had been beaten in the shack in Reed Alley might be the same bruised and battered prostitute he'd seen behind the fence at the saloon. Though he felt a certain satisfaction at having made the deduction, he was disturbed. He now had a face, and a name, to attach to a woman who obviously was enduring the most difficult and dangerous of existences.

And that woman might be the very sister of Jake Penn.

McCutcheon didn't know Penn well; their time together had been relatively brief. Even so, he could guess how devastated Penn would be to learn that his sister was involved in that kind of life. And hadn't he overheard the policeman telling Drake that Nora's own husband was behind her prostitution?

To McCutcheon, such a thing was unimaginable.

I've got to do something for her. Penn helped me for the sake of my father and mother. I can't do any less for him.

At the moment, the immediate task was to verify that Nora Jackson was Nora Penn.

Deep inside, he hoped she wasn't. It would relieve him of a burdensome responsibility if she proved to be unrelated to Jake Penn.

Already, though, he had the strongest intuition that she was. Without even trying, he'd stumbled across Jake Penn's sister. It was odd, it was unlikely . . . but that was just the way life was sometimes. Always throwing a man the last thing he expected.

If McCutcheon stood back against the side of the building on the left side of the alleyway and kept the little privy house in front of him, he found he could keep a watch on Nora Jackson's little shack without being seen himself. He stood there and kept watch for activity.

After an hour, however, he decided he might as well move on. It was nearly time for him to go to his job, and there was no sign of life around the Jackson shack at the moment. Probably no one was home.

McCutcheon was abut to leave when he saw her. She was on foot, walking slowly up Reed Alley, looking very tired. In the daylight, she seemed older than she had under the shroud of darkness.

McCutcheon squeezed back into the shadows

to make sure she did not notice him, and peered closely at her, trying to spot any possible family resemblance to Jake Penn.

The front door of the shack opened, and a black man emerged. His face was discolored, his nose swollen. McCutcheon supposed a skillet across the face would tend to do that to a man.

"There you are," the man said harshly. "What took so long?"

"I took so long," she replied. "I'm tired. I walk slow when I'm tired."

"How much he pay you?"

"The usual."

"Let's have it."

McCutcheon watched her dig into a pocket of her ragged dress and bring out money. The man snatched it and counted it quickly.

"It ain't all here. You holding out on me, woman?"

"I ain't holding out nothing."

"Then out with the rest of it!"

She dug into her pocket again, and produced a coin. She held it out to him with a trembling hand.

"I reckon it was stuck in there," she said meekly.

"Yeah. Stuck. Stuck 'cause you was going to keep it. You can't lie to me, woman. You hold out on me, and I'll smack you good. And you know I will."

McCutcheon expected some sort of defiant retort from the woman, but the man's threat seemed to deflate her. He supposed that Jackson had fulfilled enough threats through the years to cause her to take him seriously.

"I didn't do it on purpose, Zeke. I swear I didn't. It was stuck in there."

Zeke Jackson. So that was his name. Zeke Jackson, a man who prostituted his own mistreated, beaten wife and then took all the proceeds for himself, not even leaving her a dollar for herself. McCutcheon stood there in the shadows, hating him.

Zeke Jackson leaned forward and kissed Nora on the cheek, but there was no love in it. Somehow he made that cold buss seem like a threat all its own. He caressed her neck, but it was very nearly a choke. "You just always play the game fair and square with me, and you'll be just fine," Jackson said.

Go get your skillet, Nora, McCutcheon thought. *He wants a kiss, kiss him with that.*

The Jacksons went into the house. McCutcheon lingered for a few more minutes, but heard and saw nothing more.

He headed for the saloon, preoccupied and brooding.

Chapter Twelve

Things did not go well at the saloon that particular night, and they got worse the later the hour grew.

It was a night filled with whiskey and troublemakers. Before the evening was old, McCutcheon was forced to talk two drunks out of stabbing each other, and he threw out one rowdy man who, fortunately, was too intoxicated to do too much damage. On top of it all, McCutcheon had been threatened more times than he could count.

He wondered what the devil was wrong with the city of Denver this night, and why every maniac in the town had decided to visit this particular saloon.

Curtsy Drake was having plenty of trouble of his own. He'd been threatened, too, and actually dodged a knife thrust. To his misfortune, he hadn't been as adept at dodging a blow from a crippled patron's walking stick. Drake had unwittingly trodden on the toes of the man's one good foot, and the cane became a tool of vengeance across the back of his hand.

Drake's hand quickly became a swollen, discolored mess; McCutcheon suspected it was broken, though Drake denied that it was.

One thing was clear: this was an evening when Drake truly needed help running the place. So it was the worst possible time for McCutcheon to glance out the door and see none other than Zeke Jackson passing by. He was in the company of two other black men and seemed to be quite drunk, as it seemed almost everyone in this part of Denver was this night.

McCutcheon realized he had just been handed an opportunity—an ill-timed one, but an opportunity nonetheless.

Nora might be back at her house, alone. He could talk to her. Maybe find out just who she was.

He looked about. The saloon was packed with patrons. Drake was arguing with some other disgruntled customer, while at the same time trying to shoo away a prostitute who kept hovering around the doorway.

He knew he shouldn't leave the saloon. It might cost him his job, and was terribly unfair to Drake, and to Smith, the other barkeep.

But he had to do what he knew was right.

McCutcheon slipped toward the rear door. Drake was still occupied by the throng, and Smith, who was busy slinging out drinks at the bar, threw him an angry glare as he headed for the door.

McCutcheon wondered if he could leave, do his business, and return even before Drake noticed his absence.

He stepped into the night, and headed at a fast clip toward Reed Alley.

McCutcheon stood in the middle of the alley, staring at the little shack and asking himself why he was there.

But he couldn't turn back. He'd come this far. If he could find Penn's sister for him, and get her out of a bad situation . . . that would be something he could take pride in.

He gathered his courage and walked to the door. The house was dark except for a dimly burning light somewhere deep inside; just a faint glow barely visible through the dirty windows.

McCutcheon looked up and down the alley, pleased to find it empty. He knocked lightly on the door, a part of him hoping that she wouldn't answer, so he could go on his way with a clear conscience.

But he heard footsteps on the floor inside.

"Who is that there?"

It was her voice.

"My name's Jim McCutcheon." He felt very out of place. "I'm here looking for Nora Jackson."

McCutcheon heard her draw closer to the door. "Why you want me?"

"I need to . . . talk to you."

The door rattled, then cracked open; he saw a faint silhouette looking back at him. He stood there, letting her study him as best she could in the darkness.

He must have suited her, or at least not frightened her, for she soon opened the door wider. With a hip slung to one side, she looked him over; he could barely make out her smile. "You come on in, mister. I think we can give you what you want."

It took him a couple of moments to realize what she was implying, which made him feel naive. "No, no. It's not that. I just need to talk to you."

She straightened and looked at him more cautiously. This was something new for her.

She leaned her face closer, studying him. "Wait a minute. Ain't you the man who emptied them spit jars out back of Drake's saloon?"

"Yes, that was me."

"Why've you come here?"

"Look, can I come inside? This may take a few minutes to explain."

She hesitated. "Mister, if you don't want what I'm selling, then maybe it's best you don't come in."

McCutcheon had never felt so nervous. "Listen to me . . . I know he's hurt you. I know your husband beats you. I know what he's made you do to make money. I've come here to . . . I don't know. Help you, if I can." It sounded very foolish now that he'd said it aloud.

"Help me?" She actually laughed. "Why? How?"

"That's what I'd like to talk to you about. I don't know the 'how' just yet, but the 'why' part is: I want to help you for the sake of . . . listen, can I come in or not?"

"My husband might come back."

"I saw him just a few minutes ago. He was going through town with a couple of other men. They were all drunk. I don't think he'll be back soon."

She looked at him a few moments more, considering. "Come in," she finally said.

When she cranked the lamp up higher, he was startled by what it revealed.

"He's beaten you again," he said.

She stared back at him, face swollen, eyes

darkened and circled. In them he could see an
ocean-deep despair, and a look of tired resigna-
tion.

She had laid aside her practiced seductive
manner; now she seemed only frightened, small,
and girlish, even though she was long past her
young womanhood. She was also openly mis-
trusting. She stared nervously at McCutcheon
like she might dart away if he made any kind
of quick move.

"I don't understand why you're here," she
said.

"I've come because I think I met a man who
is your brother. He's looking for you."

"My brother!"

"That's right. Jake's been looking for you for
years now. He's concerned about you, and
wants to help you . . . that is, if you're really
his sister. But he doesn't know about you being
here. He's off looking in another place, thinking
you might be there, not realizing that . . ." He
cut off, realizing he was doing little more than
babbling at her. "I'm sorry. I'm going at this all
backwards. I'm a little nervous about this, you
see. And I don't have much time, because I'm
supposed to be at my job. Besides, I didn't plan
for any of this to happen." He nervously put his
hands in and out of his pockets, gripping and

releasing his folding pocket knife again and again letting it fall to the bottom of the pocket.

She was trying to find some sense in it all. "My brother wants to help me, you say?"

"Yes. He's a good man. He saved my life. I can't say I know him well, but I think very highly of him. He helped me, too, you see."

"So my brother Jake is looking for me, you say? And he wants to help me."

McCutcheon felt a thrilling sense of confirmation. She'd just called her brother by the name "Jake"! This had to be the right Nora!

"Yes. He's been longing to see you for years."

She paused and he could see the wheels of her mind turning. "Do you think Jake would take me away from here? Away from Zeke?"

"Well . . . I don't know. If he knew you were being hurt, I think he would. But he's not here, and he doesn't know you're here . . ." McCutcheon was getting embarrassed. He was mangling this terribly. Yet Nora didn't seem confused. The despair in her eyes had quickly disappeared, and they were now lighted with hope. "Your brother is Jake Penn, isn't he?" he asked, following an impulse for further confirmation. As soon as he'd said it, he realized he'd just provided her Penn's surname . . . and now he began to wonder if maybe he'd even said Jake's name earlier than she had.

So much for confirmation. *I really am doing this all wrong,* he thought.

"Yes, that's him! Jake Penn is my brother! I didn't know Jake was looking for me! I didn't even know he was still alive!"

He is."

She was growing more excited by the moment. She turned and paced back and forth before him, talking fast. "So Jake is looking for me . . . Jake will help me, maybe take me away . . . Jake wants good things for me . . ." She wheeled to face McCutcheon again. "Is Jake coming here?"

"I told you—he doesn't even know you're here. He's gone off to the high mining towns, looking for you. Last place he looked was Millrace. He'd heard you might be there."

"So he must be asking about after me."

"Yes. So far, he's found a lot of Noras. None of them the right one."

"I'm the right one. I want to see him."

"There's a problem there."

Her expression darkened. "My husband."

"That's right."

Her eyes welled. "I hate him."

"I'm not one to break up families, but Zeke Jackson is bad for you. The way he beats you, he's going to kill you, eventually. And if he doesn't, one of the men he puts you with might."

Tears ran down her face. "He makes me do it. I don't want to do what I have to do."

McCutcheon rubbed his chin. He'd thought about finding Nora, but not about what to do after he found her. Obviously he had to bring her and Jake Penn together. But how? He didn't know where Jake was. By now he might have visited all the high towns, and then moved on.

On the other hand, he might yet be there. Hunting through several towns wasn't something that could be done quickly. McCutcheon faced a predicament. A narrow period of opportunity lay before him to, just possibly, reunite Jake Penn and his sister. Yet to bring them together, he'd either have to go find Penn and bring him here to Nora, or take Nora away from her husband and search through all the high towns.

She stood close by him, looking intently into his face. "Take me away from here," she said. "Please don't leave me. Zeke's been worse lately. He's been drinking more, and angry all the time. He beats me worse when he's angry. And he's gone out drinking tonight."

McCutcheon didn't know what to do. He hadn't planned this thing through that far. Suddenly the whole affair was taking on the character of a massive responsibility, thrust upon him from outside and demanding a reaction far more immediate than he was ready to give.

It was too much, too fast. He had to think. And he had to get back to work.

"Listen, I have to leave here now," he said. "I'll talk to you again later on."

"You can't leave! He'll come back and beat me!"

"Then maybe you should leave, too. Go somewhere else."

"He'd find me. He'd hurt me . . . maybe even kill me! You got to get me away from here!"

McCutcheon, flustered, confused, and put off by the aggressiveness of her manner, backed away. "Look, I want to help you, and I will, but I can't do it all at once, and I can't do it without a plan."

"Just take me to Jake. Take me to my brother!"

"Not now. Not yet. Give me time to think!"

"There is no time!"

McCutcheon shook his head violently. "I'll come back. I'll find some way to help."

He left with her pleading to him not to go. He closed his ears to her cries and fled down Reed Alley like a man pursued.

Chapter Thirteen

McCutcheon wasn't sure how long he'd been away from the saloon. He prayed that Drake somehow, miraculously, hadn't noticed his absence, that the place had been too busy, his attention too diverted.

Upon reaching the back door of the saloon, though, McCutcheon found that miracles weren't to come his way this night.

Smith was coming out of the door just as McCutcheon reached it. In Smith's hands were rags damp with blood, it appeared to McCutcheon.

"There you are!" Smith declared. "Where the hell have you been, McCutcheon?"

McCutcheon hadn't liked Smith the first time he saw him, and his accusatory tone now made him dislike him more. He ignored the question. "Are you hurt?" he asked, gesturing at the stained rags.

"Not me. But Mr. Drake is."

McCutcheon was shocked. "What do you mean?"

"He's been stabbed," Smith explained, "trying to throw out four violent drunks with no one to help him but me. He called for you, but you were nowhere to be found."

"I had to . . . there was no way for me to be there because . . ." McCutcheon stammered away into silence, staring at the bloody rags.

Smith grunted disdainfully, and pushed past him, getting some of the blood on the rags on McCutcheon's shirt. Smith cast the rags over the fence into the same fouled backlot that McCutcheon used to dump the spittoons.

Smith stomped back toward the saloon, not even bothering to look at McCutcheon.

"Is he dead?" McCutcheon asked, dreading the answer.

"Not yet," Smith said. "He's being tended to by a doctor right now. It's thought he'll probably live, though it will be some time before he can run this business again."

McCutcheon looked through the back door at the inside of the saloon. "Where are the customers?"

"The saloon is closed. It emptied out fast after Mr. Drake was stabbed. He left me in charge. No one else was there to take over, after all."

"Yeah. Sorry."

"Where did you go, anyway?"

"I had to visit someone. It was urgent."

"So urgent you left your job at a time when even three of us weren't a sufficient staff to operate the place?"

"I'll explain it to Mr. Drake. Not to you."

"No. I'm afraid you *will* explain it to me. I'm in charge here now. Mr. Drake gave me full authority to run this business until he returns, which will be some days. *Full* authority. That includes the hiring and dismissal of employees."

McCutcheon gave Smith the coldest look he could. "In other words?"

"In other words, you may consider yourself no longer needed here."

McCutcheon sighed. Oh, well. He hadn't planned to stay long, anyway. He never stayed long anywhere. "Very well. But I am due some pay, and if I'm to be dismissed, I'll have it now."

"You'll have to discuss that with Mr. Drake. I know nothing of what he's paid you, or what may be due."

"Really? I thought you were the boss now. The man with all the answers."

"There's no need to be snide with me."

McCutcheon's temper flared. He reached out fast and grabbed Smith by the collar, and pulled him close. "I'll have my pay. I know how much I'm due. And I know where the cash box is. I'm going to go inside, open that box, and take what I'm owed. Not a cent more. You can verify the amount with Mr. Drake later. He'll confirm that I've not taken more than my due."

"If you go into that building, I'll send up an alarm for the police!"

"You do that. By the time they get here, I'll be gone. This will only take a moment."

He shoved Smith back against the wall and released him. Striding into the empty saloon, he went for the cash box beneath the bar, quickly calculated the money he was owed, and took that amount. He exited via the rear door, right past Smith.

"I'll see you pay for this!" Smith seethed, but the threat sounded feeble.

McCutcheon paid him no heed. He was through with this place and with Smith. He regretted that his parting with Drake had been on bad terms. But for now he couldn't care less about anything else. He was too distraught and angry.

He walked away from the saloon, headed nowhere in particular, just walking to work his anger out. At last he stopped, finding himself in a part of Denver he'd not been before, his brooding anger festering.

He was frustrated not only by the evening's turn of events and the loss of his job, but also by the status of his life as a whole. He was young, strong, handsome, capable . . . he should have been well situated.

He should have had his inheritance still, and not be just another impoverished drifter roaming the West.

He dwelled on such thoughts until the pressure became too much. He rammed his fist through a nearby back door window of an empty shop. The glass shattered. He drew back his fist, startled that he'd done such a thing. He examined his hand, seeing no cuts.

Well, that much was good, anyway.

In the distraction of being fired, he'd forgotten about Nora Jackson. Now she came back to mind, and he wondered if her husband had come back home yet.

Maybe he should go and check on her.

He stopped himself. Not tonight. He'd done his share for one evening. It wasn't *his* job to make up for some black-skinned prostitute's error in marrying the wrong man!

Of course, a small voice replied, *it wasn't Jake Penn's job to save your skin from Fifer and Bee either. But he did it.*

Shut up, McCutcheon thought. *Just shut up.*

He meandered about the dark streets of Denver until he had found his way again to the woodshed where he slept. He hoped that Smith wouldn't be savvy enough to think about the fact that McCutcheon's horse was still in Drake's private stable. If he did, he'd probably seize it on some grounds or another, or otherwise cause some kind of problem.

He didn't worry much; Smith wasn't very clever and probably wouldn't ever think of such a thing. Distraught, McCutcheon settled into his blankets and went to sleep.

McCutcheon awoke an hour later when the door to the woodshed jerked open and the light of a lantern spilled inside.

He sprang up to a sitting position and was instantly blinded by the lantern's glare. A man's voice said, "Here he is! I knew there was some jackass sleeping in my shed! Up from there, you! And put them hands in the air!"

McCutcheon obeyed. He could see nothing but light and darkness, and the darting movements of forms intruding into the shed. Someone grabbed him and yanked him to his feet. In moments he was outside, in the pitch of night.

The lantern went up into his face, making him squint painfully.

"What you got to say for yourself, young

man?" his captor declared. "What makes you think you can use my shed for your bedroom?"

"I'm sorry," McCutcheon said. "I didn't know."

"Didn't know what? Didn't know it was somebody's woodshed? Then you're a very stupid man."

"I didn't hurt anything, didn't take anything."

"Tell it to the law."

There were at least two men there; McCutcheon couldn't count exactly because they kept the lantern in his eyes. The second man said, "Look at him, John . . . there's blood on him."

"I'll be!" the other said. "So there is. Where'd that blood come from, young man?"

McCutcheon had forgotten about the bloodstain on his shirt, and it took him a moment to remember how it had come to be there. "There were some bloody rags from a man who'd been stabbed. It got on me."

"A man who'd been stabbed? What man?"

The other man said, "John I'll bet this is the one who cut open that darky in Reed Alley."

McCutcheon froze. "What did you say?"

Neither answered him; they spoke only to one another.

"I'll be . . . I'll bet you're right!" the one named John said. "Caught us a killer, bet you anything!"

McCutcheon could only think: *He's killed her. He came back and killed her!*

"We got to get the law, John."

"I'll guard him. You go and find—"

McCutcheon moved. He had no plan; he just acted out of instinct, with the sense that the time to run was now or there would be no other opportunity. He lunged at the man holding the lantern and pushed him onto the ground.

McCutcheon turned and took a wild, blind swing at the second man, luckily catching him on the jaw. The man went down, stunned senseless. The other man began to scramble up, and McCutcheon kicked at him as he did so, hitting him in the groin and sending him tumbling to the ground again.

McCutcheon fled without looking back.

Chapter Fourteen

McCutcheon had developed the habit of sleeping with all his clothing on, including boots, just in case he got caught and had to make a sudden run. But other than his saddle and horse, everything else he owned, from the pistol that had once been Johnny Bee's, to his extra clothes and personal effects, were still hidden back in the woodshed.

He'd not be able to get to them now. He mentally bade them goodbye and kept running, dodging up streets and down alleys, around buildings and over fences, until he had no idea where he was, and hoped no one else did either.

He shouldn't have left Nora alone. Now, he feared, Zeke Jackson had gotten to her, and knifed her to death.

Jake, I'm sorry. I should have gotten her away from there as soon as I found her.

McCutcheon fell to the ground behind a

church house, panting, trying to gather his thoughts and catch his wind again.

Nobody would find him here; he had some time to think this thing through.

After a few minutes, he'd calmed somewhat. He reminded himself that he didn't really know that Nora was the murder victim the two men had mentioned. There were other houses in Reed Alley, and no doubt other black residents. Maybe someone else there had been stabbed.

So maybe Nora was all right. The only way he could find out was to go see. But he'd be careful. There might be police crawling about the place. They might even be looking for someone of his description, if John and his friend had recovered and gotten to the police to report the intruder in the woodshed.

He pulled out his pocketwatch, but he could hear it was not ticking; it had run down. It was too dark to see it anyway. He didn't know how long it would be until morning.

What he had to do was best done unseen, and thus best done while darkness held.

He rose and began winding his way back through streets and alleys, trying to gain his bearings and figure out how to find his way back to Reed Alley before sunrise.

* * *

McCutcheon crouched in the same hidden spot from which he'd observed the Jackson's shack before his visit with Nora, and watched as the policeman Mortimer Clair and a second officer McCutcheon hadn't seen before came out the door of the cabin and stood talking. Though they had no reason to assume anyone was near, they kept their voices low, though not so low that McCutcheon couldn't hear what was said.

"So, you think she's the one?" asked the other policeman.

"She'd certainly be my top suspect," Clair replied. "Frankly, I'm not a bit surprised that this has happened. I've been expecting something along this line, as a matter of fact. Though my expectation would have been the man killing the woman, not the other way around."

McCutcheon's eyes widened as he comprehended the significance of what he'd just heard. He felt a combination of relief and horror. The woman had killed the man?

"So where do you think she's gone?"

"Good Lord, man, how could I even guess? She could be anywhere in the city. I'm certain she'll turn up soon enough."

"Unless she gets out of town."

"Indeed. And if she does, I'll not lose much sleep over it. Any man who would make a whore of his own wife is, as far as I'm concerned, deserving of exactly what our dear friend received."

"We will search for her, I assume?"

"Of course. And I expect we'll find her."

"Are we through here for tonight?"

"As far as I'm concerned we are." Clair stretched and yawned. "It's not particularly enjoyable, being dragged out of bed to come down and see some procurer who's been laid open by his soiled dove wife, you know. I get downright sentimental about sleep when I don't get enough of it."

"It's almost morning now," the other said. "Not much point in going back to bed."

"No. So I suppose it's on to breakfast for me . . . if I have the stomach for it. He was not a pretty sight, was he? She did quite a lot of surgery on him, considering she had no more than a folding knife."

The two policemen walked off together, still talking. McCutcheon stayed where he was until they were completely out of sight and earshot. Then, looking around carefully, he rose and turned to go back the way he had come—and couldn't restrain a yell of fright when he found himself face to face with another person behind him.

"Oh, please don't make a sound!" He recognized Nora Jackson's voice. "Don't draw them policeman back here on me!"

"Nora—how long have you been behind me?"

"Just a few minutes. I was hiding over there, in the attic of that store building, looking out that little window there, when I saw you. I thought it was you, anyway; I couldn't be sure in the dark. I came down so I could make sure, and to talk to you. I was surely hoping it was you, sir."

"You killed him, Nora. I heard them talking. You killed your husband!"

"Only because he was going to kill me. And I didn't mean to do it. Not really. I only wanted to hurt him enough to make him quit hitting me. I cut him more than I thought I would . . . and then I just kept cutting. I couldn't stop myself." She paused. "I used your knife. And I dropped it in there, so the police, they got it now."

"*My* knife?" McCutcheon slapped about on his person. Sure enough, the folding knife he'd carried, formerly Fifer's, was gone. He remembered fidgeting with that knife while talking to Nora in her house, lifting and dropping it repeatedly in his pocket. . . .

"Oh, no . . . I dropped it, didn't I? In your house."

"Yes, you did. I found it just as Zeke was coming home. I hid it in my skirt, so he wouldn't ask about it. When he started to hitting me, I opened it, and—"

McCutcheon swore softly. His knife, used as a murder weapon! He wondered if there was any way to trace it to him. It bore no mark to identify him . . . but how many times had he used it in the presence of Curtsy Drake, or Smith, or any of the patrons of the saloon? Not many, he didn't think, but he couldn't be sure. He'd had no reason to be careful about it.

He glanced down at his bloodied shirt and thought about the men he'd escaped from at the woodshed. They'd be talking to the police, no doubt. Inevitably the field of suspicion in the death of Zeke Jackson would widen to two: Nora Jackson, and the young white male who'd been found hiding in a woodshed with blood on his shirt, and who'd fled like a scared rabbit.

"I've got to get out of Denver," McCutcheon said. "For good."

"So do I," Nora said. "I want you to take me away from here. Take me to my brother."

McCutcheon didn't relish the idea of fleeing with anyone in tow. He wanted to be able to move fast, and look out only for himself.

Yet he couldn't deny her. To do so would be

like spitting in the face of Jake Penn, the very man to whom he owed his life.

Still, he tried to argue her out of it. "Nora, we're more likely to be caught if we run together. And they'll come up with all kinds of speculations about motives for killing your husband. They'll say I was one of the men who paid to be with you, and that we killed him together. They'll blame us both."

She began to cry. "You got to take me! I need help! I ain't a smart woman, sir! I've always had somebody taking care of me, helping me. Even Zeke, mean as he was, took care of me! I'll get caught if you don't help me! They'll lock me up in some prison for all the rest of my life, or maybe they'll hang me! Please, sir, please don't leave me here!"

McCutcheon felt like a fire was burning in his chest. He'd been in predicaments before, but never one quite like this.

"All right," he said at length. "We'll go together. And we'll head to the high towns and see if we can find Jake Penn. If we do, I'll leave you with him. If not, we go our separate ways. Is that clear?"

"Yes, sir, yes. Whatever you want . . . just don't leave me here alone!"

A light came on in a nearby window; someone in one of the other houses had heard them.

"Who's that out there?" a voice called.

"Let's go," McCutcheon said.

They ran down the alley together just as the sun began to rise in the east.

Nora had some money, to McCutcheon's surprise, cash she'd squirreled away a little at a time, without her husband's knowledge. She'd had the foresight to remember to take it before fleeing the house. She also took Zeke's pistol and gunbelt. She kept the cash herself, but gave the weapon to McCutcheon.

They managed to sneak McCutcheon's horse and tack gear out of Drake's stable without being caught and, by the light of dawn, left Denver, taking back streets. They rode on the same horse, with McCutcheon in front and Nora in back, clinging to him. They were a conspicuous pair, riding that way, and at every corner McCutcheon expected to be hailed and stopped, but it didn't happen. Somehow they made it out.

Nora had wanted to steal a second horse from Drake's stable, but McCutcheon hadn't allowed it. Yet he knew that, practically speaking, it would have been a sensible decision. They'd not be able to ride forever on one horse. They scarcely had enough money to keep themselves fed, only one pistol and a handful of ammunition, the clothes they had on their backs, and no feed for the horse beyond the one sackful they'd been able to pilfer from Drake's stable.

McCutcheon began to resign himself to the fact that he might have to turn horse thief if he was to get far enough away from Denver to feel safe, and reach the high mining towns in time to intercept Jake Penn. He'd try to avoid it, though.

He knew from hard experience what could come of horse thieving, even when a man wasn't really guilty.

It all seemed very hopeless to him as they rode through the cool morning, with the sun and Denver behind them.

This was not how things were supposed to work out. He'd wanted to become a better man. He'd wanted to help out Jake Penn just as Jake had helped him. That was all.

There wasn't supposed to have been a killing along the way.

He hoped they'd make it to the high towns quickly, and that no one would pursue them out of Denver.

Most of all, he hoped they'd get there before Jake Penn left and vanished into the endless West.

PART 2

Under Seige

Chapter Fifteen

Several weeks later, Lower Marrowbone, Colorado

Jake Penn walked very slowly, limping down a wide alley between a miners' supply store and a canvas-roofed lawyer's office, and plopped down wearily on an empty crate someone had discarded there. Leaning back against the wall of the store, he let his tired body sag like a sack of sand and exhaled slowly, his head turned slightly up and eyes closed.

He was physically and mentally worn out, and severely disappointed. He'd searched every one of the so-called high mining towns for days on end and found nothing to indicate that his Nora—or any other Nora, for that matter—had been in any of them. He supposed those children back in Millrace had given him the best information they had, but as had been the case so often in his long search, their information just wasn't quite good enough.

A lot of miles, a lot of effort, a lot of hope and prayer . . . but still no Nora.

He was beginning to wonder if he'd ever find her.

Penn rested for several minutes, then bent over and slipped off his boots. His socks were worn through at several places, his feet sore and chafed.

Penn wriggled his toes and massaged his feet for several minutes, then put the boots back on. When he straightened up again, a man was standing nearby, close to the end of the broad alley, grinning at him. He was a black man, several years older than Penn himself.

"Howdy," the newcomer said, nodding.

"Howdy to you," Penn replied. "How are you today?"

"A little tired, but not as tired as you, if looks tell the story," the man replied. He came forward, putting out his hand. "My name's Tennison. Pleased to meet you."

They shook hands. "Jake Penn."

"Yep. I knew that. Somebody told me who you were."

"Folks are talking about me, are they?"

"A little bit."

"And what are they saying?"

"They're saying that you're asking after a sister who you ain't seen since you was very young and still a slave. Is that right?"

"It is."

"Then I'm glad I found you here."

Penn perked up immediately. "You know something about Nora?"

"I wish I did. Because I understand your situation. You see, I lost a sister of my own in much the same way, a brother, too. Like you, I tried to find them years later, but I never succeeded. And I've always regretted that."

"I'm truly sorry you didn't find them," Jake Penn said.

"Well, that's how things go sometimes. I hope it will be different for you."

"I still have hopes of finding my Nora. Though I admit it's easy to grow discouraged."

"I know, I know. It's why I've sought you out."

"I don't follow you, Mr. Tennison."

"Just Tennison. No mister."

"Call me Jake. And go on with what you were saying."

"Surely, surely. Just let me set these old bones down." Tennison kicked over another empty crate near Penn, and lowered himself onto it, his joints creaking. He pulled out a knife and stick, and began to whittle off curled shavings before he spoke again.

"Jake, I told you I don't know nothing about this sister you're looking for. But it strikes me that if you're looking for her here, you must have been told she might be in Marrowbone. Am I right?"

"Not Marrowbone in particular. I heard she might be in the high mining towns somewhere. I've been searching through them all. Marrowbone here is the last one." Penn took out a cigar and offered it to Tennison, who waved it off. Penn fired it up.

"No sign of her so far?" Tennison asked.

"Not a one."

"Well, sir, are you aware of the fact that this town here is properly called Lower Marrowbone?"

"No. Does it matter?"

"It does, for it was called that to distinguish it from a different Marrowbone, the older one. It lies up Marrowbone Creek, even higher in the mountains than we are now, a good dozen miles from here."

"I never heard of it."

"Not much reason you should have. It started as a gold town, maybe ten, fifteen years ago, and died away fast after that. There was a silver strike later on, though, and revived it again for a time. But it's a dead town again now . . . almost dead, anyway."

"Almost?"

"That's right. There's been a few folks who've lived in the original Marrowbone all through the years, finding enough color to keep them in some sort of a living. And lately, I happen to know, there's been some others who've gone there. It's the first time in years that I know of that the older Marrowbone has gotten itself some new residents."

"More miners?"

"I suppose. I don't know any other reason that anybody would go there. There's always folks who get the idea that they'll find a strike that everybody else has missed, you see. I saw a whole band of horsemen going in there recently, with my own eyes."

"Why are you telling me this?"

"Because if I was you, looking for my sister in the high towns, I'd not be pleased to find out that there is one high town that I'd missed out on because I hadn't heard of it."

"Was there a woman with these people you saw going in?"

"I couldn't tell you. I was out in the mountains, hunting with my nephew, when I saw them. Up near old Marrowbone we were, and we seen them riding in. A group of people, maybe nine or ten of them. It was dusk, though, and they were a long way off."

"So there's really no reason to think you saw Nora."

"You're missing the point, my friend. The point is that there's folks beginning to poke around old Marrowbone again. Maybe your Nora is there, too."

Penn nodded, rolling the cigar between his thumb and fingers. "I understand. You'll have to pardon me. I'm a very weary man."

"Listen, none of this is my affair. You do what you want. But if I was looking for my sister, like you are, I think I'd want to at least pay a visit to old Marrowbone. If you've turned over every stone but one, why not turn that over, too?"

"Makes sense."

"So you'll go look?"

"I will. Tomorrow morning."

"Good. Good. Don't give up trying. You give up, you make it certain you'll never see her again."

Penn chuckled. "Maybe the good Lord sent you to me to tell me this. Maybe He has set up a meeting with me and Nora in Marrowbone tomorrow."

"Maybe so. But watch out for the devil along the way."

"What do you mean?"

"Just that old Marrowbone can be a dangerous place."

"How so?"

"I don't suppose you've ever heard about old man St. John and his sons."

"I haven't."

"Then I'd best tell you. St. John is a madman, and probably dangerous. He's also the man who found the first silver at Marrowbone," Tennison said. "But he got sick nigh to death before he could register his claim. He grew worse and worse, and was sure he was going to die, so he told some others about the strike. They promised him that they'd put his name in as one of the owners when they filed the claim, in case he got better. But they never done it. They took the claim for themselves. Three of them, conniving together, straight out cheated him, sure he'd never live to raise a protest."

"St. John had no family who could have made the claim for him?"

"He was a widower, but he had two sons. They were just children, though, too young to stake a claim.

"The story is that old St. John is still up there, bitter over what they done to him, still watching his old mines, ready to avenge anybody who tries to get what he sees as his. Old St. John was a fiddler all his days, the story has it, and they say you can still hear his music in the middle of the night sometimes, playing all angry and hot. Music of a man who's gone mad in his fury, because he was cheated. It's the meanest, hardest music a man can ever hear, they say. He played it every night so that the men who'd cheated him would have to hear it forever."

Jake Penn couldn't squelch his grin. "So now you're telling me spook tales!" he said. "I'm sorry to be smiling, sir. But I ain't never been one to be scared by ghost stories."

"Oh, I ain't telling no ghost stories," Tennison replied seriously.

"A cheated man haunting mines sounds like a ghost story to me."

"I didn't say St. John died, did I? I said he was sick nigh to death. But he lived . . . lived to discover he was cheated.

"He never got over it. Went mad as a mongoose after that, some say because of what had been done to him, some say because of the fevers he suffered while he was sick. Me, I say it was something that would have happened, no matter what.

"Old St. John built himself a house up there in old Marrowbone, within view of the houses of the three men who'd deprived him of his rightful share. It was there that he raised two sons. One, they say, was a hardworking fellow, level-headed and intelligent. The other was as mad as his father. Scared of the world. He hid away in that strange old house, never seeing the light of day. That's why I say old St. John's madness was something that would have happened no matter what: his son going mad, too, shows that madness runs in the St. John family, and not just caused by fever or bitterness."

"Why'd you call it 'that strange old house'?" Penn asked.

"When you see it, you'll know why. I challenge you to find a door into the place, or even a window."

"How can you get inside a house without doors?"

"Tunnels, my friend. Tunnels, dug under the hill on which the house sits. By the way, St. John kept building onto his house through the years, adding more and more to it, until it's now this big old sprawling place that crawls all over the mountain."

Penn looked at him skeptically. "You ain't telling an old drifter some loco stories, are you?"

"Not a bit of it. Seen his place myself with my own two eyes many a time, when I've hunted up around old Marrowbone."

"And the old man and his sons are still there, eh?"

"One of the sons died, I was told. I think it was the crazy one, though I don't know certainly."

"How does St. John survive, if he lost his mines?"

"Them tunnels ain't entirely for access to the house. He's found enough color to keep himself alive. That's the way it is with all the old-timers still there from the first days of Marrowbone: they find just enough to get by."

"What about the men who cheated St. John?"

"Long gone, all three of them. The mines finally gave out, and they moved away, rich. Leaving St. John behind them. Their houses all burned down right after they left."

"St. John?"

"That's the presumption." The old man put away his knife and whittling stick, and stood slowly. "Well, it's been good to meet you. You can reach old Marrowbone by following the old trail along Marrowbone Creek, which flows yonder, right by the town here."

"Thank you for the information. Good evening to you."

"Good evening."

Tennison shuffled away. When he was gone, Jake Penn rose and walked to the edge of Marrowbone Creek. On the far side was a road that widened to the south, but dwindled to a burro trail up the mountain to the north. He followed the trail with his eyes as far as he could see.

Chapter Sixteen

The trail steepened and narrowed the farther Jake Penn rode. The terrain was wild and beautiful, but it gave Penn a sobering sense of remoteness and isolation. But for the trail itself, a man could easily feel he was moving through mountain country never before explored by another human being.

Penn stopped several times, both to rest his horse and to consider whether he should turn back. He couldn't help but feel he was wasting his time. Surely Nora wouldn't be in *this* Marrowbone. He wondered if he would really find anyone there at all. Maybe old Tennison was nothing but a teller of big and fantastic stories.

Yet there was a trail, and trails led somewhere. And he couldn't say for sure, without investigation, that Nora wasn't in old Marrowbone. Tennison was right about one thing, anyway: if Penn left the high towns without exploring every one of them, even the most unlikely-seeming one, he'd always wonder if he might have come close to Nora, only to miss her out of negligence.

Marrowbone Creek spilled down the mountain to the right, paralleling the trail. It was fast, crashing over stones, filling the air with a constant roar, adding to the feral sense of this isolated region.

"I'm not going to find her, horse," he said aloud. "I got the strongest feeling that you and me are wasting our time. The only reason I had to believe she was in the high towns to begin with was the talk of children in Millrace, and it strains my mind to believe she'd ever have come along so remote a trail as this one. But on we go, me and you. May as well, hey?"

Penn only had the one horse now, having sold the one he'd taken from Jack Fifer. A drifting man like himself did what he had to do to survive. But his resources were running low again; before long, Jake Penn would have to find himself some work and rebuild his financial situation a little. And a little was all it would take; he was a master of surviving on almost nothing.

Eventually Penn had to leave the saddle and let the horse walk. It was straining hard to breathe in the thin mountain air. And the horse seemed skittish as well, which Penn couldn't account for.

Funny thing, Penn noticed. He felt a bit skittish himself. As if there was some unseen danger nearby. Just as he thought it, a huge bear, a monstrous, looming grizzly, appeared among the big rocks that stood on the other side of the creek. It roared and splashed heavily into the water, and started to come at him.

Penn yanked his rifle from its boot reflexively, for he was so surprised he was hardly conscious of what he was doing. He raised the rifle and pointed it at the charging bear.

The horse panicked and bolted, yanking free of Penn's grasp. Penn fired, and missed. Levering his rifle, he fired again, and hit the bear somewhere on its lower neck. He might as well have thrown a pebble at it for all the effect it had.

Penn turned and ran, scrambling into high, broken rocks ahead of him, hoping to find some narrow niche through which he could escape but the bear could not follow. Yet the bear raced on toward him. He wheeled and fired another shot but didn't think he hit the beast.

Penn clambered onto a big boulder and was about to slide down its far side when he saw, too late, that there *was* no other side. A long, deep gully opened up below him. He tried to stop himself, but couldn't. Teetering precariously, the bear charging at him from behind, a hard and potentially fatal fall awaiting him below, he struggled to keep his balance, and then he fell.

Penn plunged, rolling and scraping down the smooth, nearly sheer face of the stone wall, and landed hard at the bottom. He lost his rifle somewhere along the way, and bruised his hip by landing on top of his holstered pistol. There he lay, the wind knocked from him, body and mind both stunned.

But he thought: *I'm alive! I'm still alive!*

He was quite surprised by this, and pleased, though he realized quickly that the bear might make its way down and tear him to pieces at its leisure.

He tried to move one arm, then the other. He gingerly felt his sides. They were sore, but not so painful as to make him suspect he'd broken any ribs. He turned his head and looked back up the way he'd fallen. He'd had the good fortune to come down a long slope that had, to some measure, let him slide down in relatively gentle fashion.

The bear roared somewhere above.

Penn tested his legs; they moved, too. He lay there until he had caught his breath, then tried to get up.

Though he was sore, he seemed to be in one piece.

He spotted his rifle nearby, very scratched and dirtied, but not visibly bent. He picked it up and worked the lever; everything seemed to function as it should.

"Thank you, Lord," Penn muttered. "It's a miracle for sure, and I do appreciate it."

He heard the bear moving above, probably looking for some way down to him. Knowing that before long it would probably succeed, Penn scrambled along the base of the gully, searching for a way to escape. The ground below grew more shallow, and he was able to pull himself out on the far side of it before long. It hurt a little to do it, but not badly. Again Penn offered a prayer of thanks that he hadn't been broken to pieces.

He paid little heed to the direction in which he was going, wanting only to put distance between himself and the grizzly. He kept watch, wondering if the bear would come after him, and was soon convinced that he had lost the bear.

Penn sank to his haunches, leaning on the rifle, and rested for a long time.

At length Penn rose and began trying to assess where he was and what he should do. He'd lost his bearing a little, but was sure that he'd soon be able to get back on the trail again.

The worst of the situation was that his horse was gone. Though he had his rifle and pistol, a little bit of ammunition, and a few items stowed in his pockets, all his other possessions were in his saddlebags, which, like the horse and saddle, were now gone.

Best try to find his horse, he decided. And keep a wary eye out for that bear.

He wound his way through the rugged mountain country, heading toward Marrowbone Creek and the trail he'd left. The roar of the creek served as an audible guide.

Eventually he reached a level meadow several hundred yards across, and there he saw his horse, still saddled, picking at the sparse growth on the rocky ground. Penn couldn't help but grin.

He was about to walk across the clearing when he saw another man do so from a different direction. The man broke out of a stand of conifers, running very hard, pushing himself so hard he was scarcely keeping afoot. Penn froze, wondering if this man was being chased by that same cussed bear. The man glanced behind him a few times, still running, then jerked to a fast halt when he saw the horse.

Penn heard the man laugh raggedly. "Thank heaven!" the man said, gasping out the words. He made for the horse, and gave two more fast glances behind him, clearly looking for some pursuer.

"Easy, there, easy," the man said as he neared the horse, which nickered softly, still edgy. "Easy, now."

But the horse spooked again, then ran.

The man fell to his knees and sobbed aloud. It was then that Penn saw that he wasn't a man at all, but a boy still in his teens, and obviously terrified.

Penn was about to step out and find out what the situation was, but before he could, two men with rifles appeared at the edge of the clearing at about the same spot from which the running youth had emerged. Penn fell back into the rocks.

The boy turned his head, saw the men, scrambled to his feet, and ran again.

One of his pursuers dropped to his knee, raised his rifle, and fired. The blast sounded somewhat thin in the high, open atmosphere of the mountainside meadow. The running boy threw out his arms and fell.

The rifleman stood and levered in a new round. "Got him square."

"Let's go see if he's dead," the other said.

"No need. He's dead, sure as hell," the shootist replied. "I hit him through the middle of his back."

"Yeah," the other said. "Yeah. You're right. I'm tired. Let's go back and give the word to Nathan."

They turned and strode back across the meadow, traveling in the direction of old Marrowbone.

Chapter Seventeen

Penn rose from his hiding place and crossed the meadow, approaching the young man's unmoving body.

He was hardly more than a child, looking pitiful lying there sprawled and bloody and still . . .

Penn saw his bloodied back heave, just a little. He was breathing!

Penn knelt and put his face low to the ground, right by the youth's face.

"Young man, can you hear me?"

The boy murmured softly. His eyelids fluttered.

"You're hurt badly, my friend," Penn said. "I'll not lie to you about that. I don't know if I can help you, but I'll try."

The boy's eyes opened. "Parlee . . ." His voice was the weakest of whispers.

"What's that you say? Parlee?"

He nodded feebly. His skin was a pallid gray. "Roll me . . . over. Want to talk."

"It might not do for me to move you. You were shot in the back."

"Please . . . I beg you."

Penn rolled him over as gently as he could, and brushed dirt and grass fragments away from his gray face.

"Is Parlee your name?" Penn asked.

"No . . . no . . . not me. Parlee . . . two of 'em, with a gang of . . . robbers, killers . . . in Marrowbone . . . in Marrowbone." The boy fought to get out his words.

"These Parlees, are they the men who shot you?"

"Yes. Trying to get . . . away. They shot my father . . . I wanted to get help for him . . . they chased me." For just a moment he seemed to be regaining just a little strength, drawing from his anger.

"Are these Parlees the same outlaws who've made that name so famous?"

"Yes."

Penn thought hard, and took a guess. "They've taken over Marrowbone, maybe? Hiding there? Is that it?"

The young man nodded with surprising vigor, but the effort took something out of him. His face grew ashen.

"Why?" Penn asked.

The young man tried to answer, but couldn't seem to get it out.

Penn took another stab at it. "Because it's remote? Cut off?"

A very weak nod came in reply. The young man shut his eyes and grimly summoned up some strength.

"But there's more. One of them is hurt," he whispered. "Marcus Parlee . . . shot . . . by his own brother. The Parlee brothers . . . divided. Fighting among themselves. Two of them . . . in old Marrowbone now. The third . . . not there."

There were so many more questions about these Parlees that Penn could ask, but one question loomed over them all.

"Son, tell me . . . is there a Negro woman in Marrowbone, name of Nora?"

The boy's lips barely moved, but no sound was emitted as he struggled to speak. "Nora . . . near my age, but a few years younger," Penn pressed.

The boy's mouth quivered, his throat made a raspy noise, but he failed to form words.

"Please," Penn said, grasping the young man's hand. "If you can't speak, squeeze my hand if she's there."

The young man stiffened, his hand squeezing tight, then he relaxed utterly. His palm slipped from Penn's grasp.

Penn stood, looking down at the young shooting victim, and wondered if that final squeeze had been a confirmation, or simply the final spasm of a dying body.

He looked around, hoping to spot his horse, and get back to his saddlebags and supplies. But it was nowhere to be seen.

"Wish I had the means to bury you, young man," he said to the dead youth. "Best I can do right now is drag you into yonder rocks, and maybe later come back and bury you proper."

He picked up the dead young man and carried him slowly toward the jumbled stones.

About the same time Jake Penn was fleeing from the rampaging grizzly bear, Jim McCutcheon and Nora were nearing Lower Marrowbone.

In the weeks since they'd left Denver, they had visited each high town inquiring after Jake Penn. In the bustling, ever-shifting population of mining towns, this would have been like searching for a single bird out of a huge, circling flock, if not for the fact Penn himself had been a conspicuous searcher.

Penn's inquires after Nora had made him far more noticeable and memorable than he would have been otherwise. The fact that he was also black only made him all the more easily recollected by those he'd encountered.

McCutcheon had discovered that by visiting saloons, cafés, street-corner bootblacks, and other such places, he'd been able to pick up Penn's track quite easily and follow it remarkably well. People remembered the black man with all the questions about his lost sister.

Though it had been easier than they had anticipated to find and follow Penn's trail, McCutcheon and Nora had yet to catch up to him. Penn was always at least one town ahead.

Now, as McCutcheon and Nora Jackson entered Lower Marrowbone, there was cause to be particularly optimistic. This was the last of the high towns, the only place left for Penn to come. Penn was no more than a day ahead, McCutcheon believed, and probably closer. He and Nora had closed the gap of time and distance quite handily.

McCutcheon led his horse down the middle of the street, Nora astride it. This had been their traveling method all along the way through the towns they had visited: Nora in the saddle, McCutcheon on foot. As a result, the young man had built up some powerful leg muscles and dropped at least ten pounds since they'd started their journey.

McCutcheon glanced up at Nora. "Are you

happy that you might actually meet your brother today?" he asked.

"Oh, yes," she replied enthusiastically. "I want to see my Jakey. I can't wait to lay eyes on him again."

McCutcheon smiled at her, but his inner feelings were far different than he revealed.

Now that he'd spent many days in Nora's company, McCutcheon was not at all sure now that he wasn't being lied to every time she opened her mouth.

He couldn't prove anything, for she was a clever woman and gave vague answers that McCutcheon could question, but never quite refute.

After all, what did he know about Jake Penn's childhood, beyond what few details Penn had told him in their brief time together? And how could he say with any certainty that the traumas of the kind of life Nora had lived really had caused her to fail to remember most of her early life experiences, as she claimed it had? Even cause her to hesitate when he asked her what her parents' names were? Her seeming ignorance of almost everything to do with Jake Penn was entirely reasonable, considering that she hadn't seen him since her childhood.

Nonetheless, it was growing harder all the

time for him to feel sure that Nora Jackson had ever been Nora Penn.

One thing, though, spoke in favor of the idea: the fact that she continued to stay with McCutcheon at all, and press on with the search. If she was a fraud, it was odd that she had no seeming concerns about finding the man who could expose her. If she was a fake, then why hadn't she abandoned McCutcheon as soon as they were safely out of Denver?

McCutcheon had presented this argument to himself many times, eager to be convinced by it; he didn't want to believe he was wasting his time and taking risks for nothing.

McCutcheon chuckled: "Jakey, eh? That's what you called him?"

"That's right. Jakey. I do love my Jakey."

Skepticism overwhelmed McCutcheon once more, and he thought: *Bilge. You've never laid eyes on "Jakey" in your life. You're a fraud, and when Jake Penn sees you, he'll send you packing. And I'll be glad to see you go.*

"I'm tired, Jimmy," Nora said. She'd taken to calling him Jimmy shortly after they left Denver, and hadn't desisted despite his strong hints that the nickname annoyed him, as it always had in his boyhood. "You reckon there'll be a real bed to sleep in tonight? I'm tired of the ground, and smokehouses, and barns."

"Maybe 'Jakey' will put you up in a hotel," he said sarcastically. She'd not seemed to notice.

"Oh, I hope he will put me in a good place!" she replied. "I'm sure he will. He'll make sure his Nora has all the good things she's missed all her life."

"You need to keep in mind that Jake Penn is far from a wealthy man," McCutcheon said. "He's a drifter, like me. And just as poor."

"Jakey will take care of me," she said, confident. "He'll work hard to take care of his Nora."

His Nora. McCutcheon curled his lip, disdainful. *Yes, Nora, but first off you'll have to convince him that "his Nora" is who you are . . . and I rather wonder if you'll be able to do it.*

McCutcheon led the horse to a hitching rail and tied it off with Nora still in the saddle.

"There's a barbershop there," he said, nodding toward a nearby building. "I'm going to go in and ask if anybody's seen Jake."

"I'll sit right here and wait," Nora said.

"You do that."

Chapter Eighteen

McCutcheon was just stepping up onto the boardwalk in front of the board-and-batten barbershop when a group of about a half-dozen riders came around a nearby corner, riding far too fast and carelessly for a busy town street. People scattered, some yelled in fright, others cursed. The riders came on, heedless, drawing attention from everyone on the street and seemingly glad they were.

McCutcheon felt a chill. These were hardcases. Dangerous men. All it took to see it was a glance. He'd run across this kind before, and knew the best policy was to stay clear of them. Probably drifters, like he was, but of the roughest variety.

They stopped their horses and dismounted before a saloon on the far side of the street from where Nora sat perched in the saddle. They had smirking grins, ugly faces, abundant whiskers, and plenty of trail dust on their clothing. They grinned hungrily at every woman they saw. One of them spotted Nora, pointed, and nudged a companion.

McCutcheon, not wanting to stare at them, turned and headed on into the barbershop.

The barber was just finishing clipping the curled locks of a nattily dressed man in a suit. A lawyer, McCutcheon figured. Mining towns crawled with them.

"Prime job!" the suited man declared as he inspected himself in a mirror. He dug into his pocket and brought out the barber's pay. "Keep the change for yourself, Walter. I'll see you again next week."

When the man was gone, the barber turned to McCutcheon. He'd been tipped nicely and was in a good mood.

"That's McDale. A banker here. Comes in every week for a cut, and pays me double every time. A good customer, McDale is."

McCutcheon grinned. "I'd say so. I had him figured for a lawyer, though a banker fits, too."

The barber was eyeing McCutcheon's unruly, untrimmed hair, and the several days' worth of unshaven whiskers bristling his face. "Shave and a haircut?" he asked. "I'll make you look like a banker yourself."

"Later. Right now I'm just after some information. I'm trying to track down a man, a Negro. Fifty years old, somewhere thereabouts. His name's Jake Penn, and I believe he's been in town here, and maybe still is."

"Jake Penn . . . name doesn't ring a bell with me."

"It wouldn't. But he'd have come asking if you'd seen a woman name of Nora. His sister. He's been looking for her."

The barber's eyes lighted up as soon as the name "Nora" was spoken, and McCutcheon knew he'd struck paydirt. Good old conspicuous Jake Penn! It would be hard *not* to find the man's trail.

"Ah, yes! Him! I believe I did see him. Yesterday, I think. Yes, that's it. He came to the door and asked me if I knew of a Negro woman hereabouts by name of Nora. Which I didn't. But I do remember him now."

McCutcheon said, "Well, I think I've found his Nora. A woman who claims to be her, anyway. I owe Jake Penn a sizable favor, and hope to bring her to him. Do you know where he might be now?"

"I'm afraid not," the barber said. "After I told him I knew nothing of his sister, he thanked me and left."

In the corner of the barbershop was a clump of what McCutcheon thought was a heap of rags. As it was, he didn't pay much attention to the heap at all, until it suddenly moved. McCutcheon was startled, and even the barber jumped back in surprise.

The rag heap was in fact a black man, sleeping beneath a big coat thrown across him like a blanket.

"Tennison, I swear, you startled me!" the barber said. "I'd clean forgotten you were there. You ought to take to snoring or something so I won't forget you when you're sleeping in here."

Tennison ignored the barber and looked straight at McCutcheon. "Did I hear you say you was looking for Jake Penn?"

"Yes. Do you know where he is?"

"Well, I know where he *likely* is, for 'twas me who told him where he ought to go just yesterday. I think he's gone to Marrowbone. Probably went up there this morning, matter of fact."

McCutcheon was puzzled. "But *this* is Marrowbone."

"No, not really," the barber said, grinning. "It's a source of confusion for many folks. This, properly speaking, is Lower Marrowbone, though these days most folks just simply call it Marrowbone. But the actual, original town of Marrowbone is about a dozen miles up the creek, higher in the mountains. It's right near being a ghost town today."

"And that's where Penn is?"

"I told him that if he was me looking for my sister, I'd want to check them both before I gave up. I presume he's gone to do that, though I can't say it certain," Tennison replied.

"Why would he want to check in a ghost town, though?" McCutcheon asked.

"It ain't completely a ghost town, sir. There are some folks still there, and even a few more I saw going in recently."

"I hadn't heard that," the barber said.

"Oh, yes. It's true. I seen 'em with my own eyes."

McCutcheon asked, "How do I get to this other Marrowbone?"

"Just follow the trail by the creek up the mountain, sir, and you'll get there," Tennison said.

McCutcheon was beginning to feel invigorated. This seemed the strongest, freshest lead he'd found yet. "I'll go there," he said. "But if you see Jake Penn in town here, I'd appreciate it much if you'd tell him not to leave. Tell him that Jim McCutcheon is looking for him, and he's got a woman with him who may be Nora."

"I'll tell him, sir."

"You ready for that shave and haircut now?" the barber asked.

"Later on," McCutcheon said. The truth was

he couldn't afford any barbering, being down to his last pennies. "Thanks to you both."

He left the barbershop and leaped from the boardwalk to the street, ready to trot across to tell Nora the news. But he stopped as soon as he landed on the street, for when he'd looked up toward her, what he saw set off an instant alarm in his mind.

Trouble was something he didn't need right now, but it looked like he'd just found it.

Nora was still in the saddle, but she was no longer alone. One of the gang of rowdies who had ridden into town minutes ago was with her, leaning against the hitching rail, talking to her with a leering smile on his face. One of his hands balanced on the rail, the other on the side of the horse, near Nora's thigh.

Nora was doing her share of talking and smiling too, McCutcheon noticed.

He walked slowly toward the pair; the man was the first to notice him. His expression hardened as McCutcheon neared. For a moment he evaluated McCutcheon, then resumed his look of smirking belligerence.

McCutcheon wished he hadn't stashed that pistol of Zeke Washington's in the saddlebag, out of reach. Then again, maybe it was good that it was. He was looking for Jake Penn, not a fight.

Nora then noticed McCutcheon, and her expression changed, too. The smile vanished.

"Something I can do for you, partner?" the man asked McCutcheon.

"Not a thing that I can think of," McCutcheon replied very casually, almost friendly, hoping this situation would simply defuse itself. He looked up at Nora. "Ready to move on?"

"You two together, are you?" the man asked.

"Just traveling companions," McCutcheon said. "Good day to you, sir."

"Yeah. I know about traveling," the man said. "I've done a bit of traveling with this lady myself. She travels real good, this one does."

McCutcheon stared at him. "I'm hoping nothing you say is intended to disrespect this lady."

Grinning, the man laid his hand on Nora's thigh. "No disrespect intended."

Marvelous, McCutcheon thought. *We couldn't just ride into town and out again. We had to run into this troublemaker.* "I'm asking you to move your hand, sir."

The man slid his hand farther up Nora's thigh. "That what you mean?"

McCutcheon stared at him. "Get your hand off the lady."

"Lady!" the man said, snorting. "This ain't no

lady. This here woman's just a whore from Denver."

McCutcheon's fist caught the man squarely on the chin, driving him back. The man's hip caught the corner of the hitching rail and caused him to pirouette and collapse on the edge of the boardwalk. He swore as he started to rise up again, groping under his coat for what McCutcheon figured was a hidden pistol. McCutcheon drove another punch into his jaw, then another. The man collapsed, unconscious.

Nora began to wail, whether out of shock or because she didn't like what McCutcheon had just done, McCutcheon didn't know.

He looked up at her, shaking the pain out of his hand. That man had one stone-hard chin.

Tears streamed down her face. "He was one of the bad men," she said. "He was one of the ones that Zeke made me lie with. I hate him! I hate all of them who done such things to me!" She buried her face in her hands.

"I could tell," McCutcheon said. "That beaming smile of yours spoke strongly of your deep hatred of the man."

"You're making fun of me!"

"Maybe I am. Because I can't figure out what to think about you."

He looked across the street. A couple of the other toughs, companions of the man he'd struck, were standing there watching. He noticed the guns holstered at their sides. It came to mind that perhaps he'd just bought himself a problem bigger than he was equipped to handle, and wondered if he should dig out Zeke Washington's pistol. But to his surprise, the watching men merely grinned at him; one even gave a friendly salute. What he'd done obviously had amused them greatly.

Perhaps that wasn't all that surprising, once McCutcheon thought about it. These men looked like the kind who would slap their thighs and laugh if a man fell down and poked his eye out on a stick.

"We'd best get away from here," McCutcheon said to Nora. "When our friend comes to, he won't be a happy man, and frankly, I'm not in the mood to mess with him. Besides, I think I've found out where Penn is."

Nora was mad at him for what he'd said earlier, and refused to reply.

The little altercation had drawn a lot of attention, and McCutcheon felt uncomfortably conspicuous as he walked the horse up the street, Nora astride it. She began to murmur and wipe away tears. McCutcheon knew what was coming. This was a prelude to another wailing festival—she'd conducted several since they left Denver.

"Hold on there, my friend!"

The call came from one of the rowdies who'd watched McCutcheon knock out their companion.

McCutcheon turned, ready to fight again if need be. But the man who'd heralded him was grinning as he approached.

"Ain't never seen anybody deal with Joe so sweetly as that," the man said. "I got to admire your grit. Most back down from Joe, and you faced him bravely. But let me give you some advice: Joe ain't going to find it amusing at all when he wakes up. He'll not forget what you've done to him. And he'll not forget your face. Don't ever let him lay eyes on you again. If you do, he'll kill you. I've seen him do some mighty bad things to men for a lot less than what you did." The man patted McCutcheon on the shoulder. "Just a friendly word of warning."

McCutcheon turned away and continued on. The pair continued across the street to deal with their fallen companion.

Nora started weeping outright. McCutcheon knew she'd go on for a long time; her well of tears was infinitely deep.

McCutcheon glanced up at her, annoyed. "Can't you at least hold your crying until we're out of town?"

That only made her howl all the louder.

Chapter Nineteen

Outside of town, McCutcheon tried to ignore Nora's wailing, but finally it became too much.

"Get down," McCutcheon said, halting the horse.

She looked down at him, sniffing and confused.

"What?" she said.

"Get down," I said.

She did, looking afraid. He grasped her shoulders and stared into her face. "Nora, I want you to tell me something: Is anything you've ever told me the truth?"

"What?"

"You heard me. I want to know if you've ever told me the truth about anything. About who you are, about what you've done, about the circumstances of your husband's death, about Jake Penn . . . all of it."

Tears streamed down her face. "Of course I've told you the truth."

"Is that right? You know, I just don't believe it. I think you've been lying to me all along."

"Why you saying that?"

"Because of all the contradictions in things you've said. Because every time you can't remember things from your childhood that most anybody would remember, you just cover it up by saying you've had such a hard life that all your memories just washed out of you. Because when you saw me coming while that hardcase was talking to you, you put on this solemn and sad manner, yet just a second before you'd been grinning at that man like he was your best friend and maybe a lot more than that. Which Nora is you? Which one is the truth?"

Somewhere underneath her weepy veneer, haughtiness flickered briefly. "What's wrong? You jealous of him because I smiled at him like I don't smile at you?"

For some reason, that made McCutcheon so angry that he literally couldn't speak. The image of himself slapping her, hard, played through his mind, an image that satisfied him immensely. But he resisted the impulse.

"Listen to me," he said. "I didn't have to involve myself with you. I didn't have to help you get safely out of Denver. And I don't have to take you to your brother . . . if Jake really is your brother. And of that I'm no longer certain, because, looking back, it seems to me that the first time we met, I fed you every clue you needed to allow you to make a good pretense of being Nora Penn. I've been good to you, and I expect you to be good to me in turn."

She pondered a moment, and her tears abruptly stopped. Her grin was unsettling. She reached out and stroked his face.

"Is *that* what you're asking me? You could have had me be good to you anytime at all along the way. All you had to do was ask me."

He was appalled. "No! That's not what I'm talking about. I want you to tell me that I'm not wasting my time taking you to Jake Penn. I want you to tell me, truthfully and honestly, if you're really his sister."

She pulled back from him, embarrassed that she'd misunderstood his intentions. "I am Jake's sister. I swear it."

"How is it, then, that you can remember Jake Penn, when you couldn't even recall the names of your parents? How is it that Jake didn't get washed out of your memories along with everything else from your early days? I simply don't understand, Nora. It makes me think you're using me for protection and lying to me about who you really are. And it makes me think maybe you have in mind to do the same with Jake Penn, once we find him."

"Jakey's my brother! I know he is! I don't know how I remember that and not other things . . . I just do. I could never forget him."

"You swear to me?"

"I swear!"

"He'll know if you're lying, Nora. I can't know, but he will."

Something that might have been veiled concern darkened her eyes. She said, "How could he know? It's been a lot of years. People don't look the same when they're children as when they're grown."

"He'll know. I'm sure of it."

She paused, growing irritable, then said petulantly, "If he's that smart, he'll know I'm the real Nora. And if he ain't, and he turns me out, maybe I'll I just find Joe again, and let *him* take care of me."

"That's what this is all about to you, isn't it? You just want somebody to take care of you."

She looked down her nose at him.

"Who's Joe anyway?" McCutcheon asked.

"He's the man you knocked out back in town, that's who he is."

"I see. The man you hated so much that you beamed at him like a full moon."

"Don't you mock me. If Joe Parlee gets his hands on you, he'll have you dead."

McCutcheon paused. "Joe Parlee?"

"That's right. You heard of him, I can tell."

By now, there was probably no American west of the Mississippi who hadn't heard of Joe Parlee, his two brothers, and the gang of outlaws they'd surrounded themselves with.

Joe Parlee! McCutcheon couldn't believe it. He'd just knocked cold one of the most feared gunmen in the West, one of a gang reputed to have committed at least a dozen murders and uncounted robberies, assaults, and other heinous crimes.

McCutcheon felt vaguely ill. Trouble with the Parlees was trouble he didn't need.

"Come on," he said. "Let's start moving again."

"You afraid? Is that it? You afraid Joe is going to show up behind us and kill you dead?"

For the first time since he'd known her, McCutcheon felt sure he was seeing the authentic Nora Jackson. The bitter, cruel edge of her words and sentiments fit what he would expect of a woman who had been misused all her years.

He didn't want to talk anymore. He had her climb back in the saddle, and they moved on toward old Marrowbone.

*   *   *

Jake Penn climbed slowly up the steep hillside, trying not to make any noise and glancing continually about, worried about unseen watchers. He heard voices on the far side of the hill—the sounds of a woman weeping inconsolably, and a male speaking loud and angry.

Penn had approached Marrowbone very carefully, hardly taking a step without first thoroughly examining the land around him. He'd heard of the Parlees, and knew how dangerous they were. He only wished he'd been able to find out more about the situation here before the young boy had died.

Above him on the hilltop stood the remains of a house that had been burned. It had been a large house. Nothing was left now but the foundation and assorted charred rubble, along with a couple of outbuildings at the sides. Weeds and brush had overgrown the ruins.

Penn crossed the overgrown yard to the back of the burned-out house and paused, listening to the noises from beyond the hill. Walking among the house's ruins, he crept around, keeping close to the foundation wall, then rose slowly at a place where a bit of charred wall remained. He looked through a gap in the wood and saw a surprising scene below.

A small crowd of people were clustered on

the street in a group. One woman was on her knees, the head of a reclining man in her lap. She stroked his hair, leaning over him; Penn's impression was that she was weeping.

A few armed men stood around them in a rough circle.

Strutting around the perimeter of the group carrying a shotgun was a man of about thirty. It was his voice that Penn had heard from across the rise. From his manner and the general look of the scenario, Penn saw that this man dominated the situation below.

Penn settled himself as comfortably as he could and began to listen, and think.

He knew already that the infamous Parlees had taken over the little near-ghost town, and that one of the brothers was injured in some fashion. The man with his head in the woman's lap was shirtless, and bandaged heavily across the chest, the gauze soaked with blood.

The wounded Parlee brother? Penn figured not. More likely the strutting man with the shotgun was a Parlee and the man on the ground was one of the townsfolk.

Penn would bet that it was the father of the boy who'd been gunned down. *They wounded my father*, the poor boy had said.

Intrigued as he was by the drama below, Penn didn't forget what had brought him here in the first place. He scoured the crowd for anyone who might be Nora. There wasn't a single black face among the throng.

But he didn't feel disappointed. Considering the kind of things going on in this town, he didn't want his sister to be here.

Chapter Twenty

Now that he was closer, Penn could almost hear the words spoken below. When suddenly the wind shifted in his direction, all at once he could hear them with clarity.

". . . and it wasn't our intention that anyone should be hurt of killed here," the strutting speaker was saying. "You were told from the outset that cooperation would bring safety, and that resistance or running would get you killed. Did you think we were lying to you? Did you?"

The speaker stopped pacing and turned to face the kneeling woman. He stalked toward her and the little crowd parted to let him in. He stood over the woman and shouted, "I asked you a question! Did you think we were lying to you?"

"No!" the woman said. "No, no!"

"I wasn't asking *you*, you old cow," the speaker said. "I was talking to this fool here."

He pivoted and kicked the bandaged man, who jerked and cried out.

"Still with us, are you?" the shotgun-toter said. "You won't be for long, my friend. Not as badly as you're wounded. You'll be as dead as your son before long." He leaned over so he could speak directly into the man's face. "Did you hear me? I said your son is dead. He was killed while running away, trying to get help for his poor old shot-up pappy! And why were you shot up, Mr. Wilbur Mason? Because you tried to fight back. What a fool you are!"

"You're cruel!" the woman screeched. "You're Satan! You're the devil himself, damn you!"

The man with the shotgun laughed again. "And don't forget it!" He wheeled about, glaring at the others.

Up in the burned-out house, Penn was seriously wondering what would happen if he took careful aim with his Winchester and blew off this cruel boaster's head, right in front of his own men and his victims. It was an engaging fantasy, but one he couldn't make a reality without greatly endangering the innocent people nearby. There were also enough armed men down there to see him dead even if he killed strutting Satan down there.

Penn wasn't one to follow the exploits of outlaws, as some did, but the Parlees were sufficiently famous for him to guess, with reasonable certitude, that Mr. Shotgun was Nathan Parlee. Hadn't one of the bad men who shot the young boy mentioned the name of Nathan as they returned to Marrowbone?

Penn tried to recall the other Parlee names. Marcus, the eldest, and the other . . . Joe. That was it. Joe Parlee.

Nathan Parlee moved back to the perimeter of the group and fell into a long, dramatic silence; Penn got the strong impression the man was doing a serious acting job, posturing and very much enjoying playing the role of tormentor.

Penn despised him.

Nathan Parlee spoke again. "I think our point has been made clear," he said to the people.

His point, Penn thought. *He wounds a father and murders a son, and to him it's making a "point."*

"We are here for a time, my brother and me and our associates here, and as long as we are, you'll obey us completely," Nathan said. "You'll not try to hurt us, and won't try to run. When we say jump, you'll jump. If you are foolish like poor old Wilbur there, and try to counter us, you'll wind up like he is. If you run, you'll wind up dead like his little boy. What was his name? Come on! Speak up, someone. Who was the young fool?"

"Kale," someone in the crowd said. "Kale Mason."

The woman beside the injured man wailed suddenly. "He's gone!" she said, face turning to the sky. "Wilbur's *dead*! I've lost my son, and now I've lost my husband!"

She laid the bandaged man's head gently on the ground and rose to her feet. Pushing out of the middle of the group, she raised a trembling finger and aimed it at Nathan Parlee's face. "You'll pay for this!" she said. "God will judge you for killing my husband and my son, Nathan Parlee! He'll send avenging angels against you and take your soul to hell!"

Lord, Penn prayed, *I'll volunteer for the job.*

One of the armed outlaws raised his rifle and pointed it toward the woman's head. Nathan Parlee waved him down. "No," he said. "No reason for that. This woman has reason to be grief-stricken."

"You'll die, Nathan Parlee! You'll burn in hell forever!"

"Perhaps so," Nathan said. "But between now and then, there'll be a hell of a lot of good living." He grinned at her.

She went after him; two of Nathan Parlee's underlings pulled her away and shoved her down. She lay in a semiseated posture, weeping, until she crawled back to where her dead husband lay. She wrapped her arms around his neck and sobbed over him.

Penn thought it was one of the saddest sights he'd ever seen.

"Move 'em back to the church with the others," Nathan Parlee said to the men around him.

The people were herded off toward the north, two of the men bearing Wilbur Mason's corpse. Penn looked around the town from his vantage point. It was as patternless as any mining town, more so, actually, as the land on which it stood was unusually hilly. All across the hillsides sat various squat huts, cabins, and interestingly, two more burned-out husks of much bigger houses like the one in which he hid.

The other two houses of the men who'd cheated St. John, Penn thought.

But where was the house of St. John himself?

He couldn't find it. He only saw jumbles of little, rugged dwellings, huts and sheds on a hillside, jammed close together.

Wait a minute . . .

As he studied some of these closer, he realized that one seeming group of small huts was actually a single, interconnected unit. It was quite a hodgepodge, log huts linked with clapboard structures, cabins and shacks all pinned together, with roofs at different levels. All in all, the place indeed looked like the work of a mad-man. It covered almost an entire hillside.

It was surely the St. John house.

Penn wondered if St. John himself, and his surviving son, had been among the little group of captives he'd just seen, a group now being herded up a hillside toward a broad, low-roofed building with a rough steeple atop it.

Penn watched as the people were forced in-side the church. He knew the population of Marrowbone was small, but he had to believe there were more people than he'd seen. Where were the others? Already in the church, he sup-posed. Maybe the smaller group who'd been brought down to the street had been singled out for some reason. Troublemakers. Resisters. Like the now-deceased men of the Mason family.

Penn changed his position, sitting back against the inside of the foundation wall, think-ing. Obviously he couldn't just walk away from this. What he'd seen had infuriated him. It was cruel, wrong.

But what could he do? How could he help these people?

He could go back to Lower Marrowbone and try to round up some official law, get a posse formed . . .

A word came to mind: *bloodbath*. Let a posse sweep in here, and that's what would happen.

The Parlees were famous for their cruelty and willingness to resist violently, and surely they wouldn't surrender readily with so many hostages in their hands.

He was one man, alone, against a gang of desperados. And he had no idea what to do.

PART 3

Counterattack

Chapter Twenty-one

"I got to stop," Nora said, breaking a silence that had lasted fifteen minutes.

"Why?"

"You know why."

"Nora, how many times are we going to have to stop for this? If you'd drunk a gallon of water, I could understand it. But this stopping every ten minutes is—"

"Listen, I'm just excited, all right? I'm going to be seeing Jakey again."

Excited, or edgy because her charade was nearing its end? McCutcheon had to wonder.

"Very well," McCutcheon said, sighing. "Go ahead. There's a thick stand of trees yonder. I'll head up this rise and wait for you."

Nora dismounted and headed for the grove. McCutcheon led the horse up the rise, wondering how long it would be until they saw Marrowbone.

That question was answered as soon as he topped the rise. Spread before him, previously cut off from view by the hill, was the town itself. There was no pattern to it, no beauty, all of it unpainted, ragged and decrepit . . . but a town. It was Marrowbone, to be sure. McCutcheon was relieved. At last they'd arrived!

And maybe, soon, he'd be free of Nora. Despite all his doubts, he hoped that Nora would prove to be Penn's sister after all. Penn would gratefully take her under wing, and McCutcheon would be blessedly free. Broke, worn-out, ragged, and probably unjustly wanted by the Denver law . . . but still free.

It sounded like paradise.

McCutcheon was about to turn back and yell to Nora that they were nearly there, but he noticed something that made him hesitate.

Three men suddenly appeared on the road, looking back at him with great interest, and talking to one another.

They were armed, and from every aspect of their movement and posture, he saw that his arrival was generating significant concern.

Why the weapons? McCutcheon was worried.

He backed up a little, but not enough to be out of the gunmen's sight. Turning his head, he called back, "Nora! Don't come out just yet."

"What?"

"I said, don't come out. Wait where you are."

"What's wrong?"

"I ain't quite sure yet."

The gunmen were headed his way at a trot, making no effort to hide their weapons.

Maybe these were lawmen of some kind, looking for a criminal believed to be around Marrowbone. Maybe they were hunters. Maybe there was a rabid animal on the loose. Several possible explanations ran through his mind, but none of them seemed very likely.

McCutcheon wished he hadn't let them see him.

"You there!" one of the men yelled. "Hold where you are!"

McCutcheon glanced back. Nora was coming out of the trees cautiously, watching him with concern. "What is it, Jimmy?"

"Go back and hide," he said, as loudly as he dared. "Keep still, keep very quiet, and don't let them see you."

"Who?"

"Men, coming my way, with guns. I can't talk anymore."

In less than two seconds, she was out of sight again.

As the gunmen neared, McCutcheon had the same instinctive sense of wariness he'd felt about Joe Parlee and his companions back in

Lower Marrowbone. These men were trouble, and it was too late for him to hide, too late to run.

Penn was still in his hiding place when he saw the three gunmen appear on the road below, looking back up the road to where it first entered the town at the crest of a hill. Penn looked and saw a lone figure standing beside a saddled horse, the reins in his hands.

Poor fellow, Penn mused. *You picked the wrong time to come to Marrowbone.*

Penn squinted, looking at the man. "Great day!" he muttered softly. "Could that really be . . . ?"

It was. Even from far off, he could tell. The man at the end of the road was Jim McCutcheon.

Penn watched, shocked and horrified, as the gunmen surrounded McCutcheon. One took the horse, while another searched McCutcheon closely, making him put his hands up. In moments they had McCutcheon marching up the road at gunpoint. As they passed beneath Penn's hiding place, he could see that McCutcheon looked utterly confused, and very worried.

And well you should be, Penn thought. *Just wait until you find out who it is who's got you prisoner.*

Penn marveled that McCutcheon had come here. What in the world could have lured him

to such a remote, unlikely spot as old Marrowbone? Had McCutcheon been following him?

If he had, he'd kept it secret, for Penn had
been on the move between the high mining
towns for many days. Why would McCutcheon
follow him in secret?

Maybe he hadn't, Penn considered. Maybe
this was just another chance crossing of paths.

Whatever it was, it made no difference. Penn
now had all the more reason to get involved in
what was happening here. No longer were the
people held by the Parlees purely a gaggle of
strangers. Now one of them was someone he
knew, someone he still felt an obligation to help.

Penn watched, dismayed, as they led McCutcheon toward the church-turned-prison for the
entire population of the tiny mining town.

Oh, Lord, he prayed, *how in the world am I
going to deal with this? What in the world can one
man do?*

He had only one advantage he could think of,
and that was that they didn't know he was here.

As advantages go, that didn't strike him as
the best he could have. An army of trained
marksmen at his side and somebody experienced in negotiating with criminals would have
been a much better choice.

Violent barking erupted behind Penn, startling him. He twisted his head and saw a huge,

black dog racing toward him, snarling and gnashing its teeth ferociously.

Penn froze, trapped in a terrible situation. If he ran, he'd be seen by the outlaws below, who were still heading up the hill toward the church with McCutcheon. If he remained, he'd be torn apart by this dog. If he fired at it, he'd draw the attention of the men below.

There was no time for much reflection. The dog, which had come bursting out of the woods behind him, was positioning itself for a final snarling spring at him. If it brought him down, it would probably tear out his throat.

Penn threw his rifle to his shoulder and fired.

Over at the church, Jim McCutcheon and the men guarding him wheeled and looked back, trying to see where the shot had come from.

"Get him inside," one of the men said to another. Turning to the third, he said, "Let's go investigate."

As he was being pushed through the door, McCutcheon finally zeroed in on the spot where the ruckus came from. Over in the burned remnants of what had apparently once been a large house, he saw a dog running furiously at a man.

It was hard to tell, but the man appeared to be black. McCutcheon didn't have a chance to look closer before he was shoved roughly through the church door.

It had been only a moment's glimpse, but McCutcheon felt that it was certainly Jake Penn he'd seen.

The shot had missed the dog, but the violent report startled it badly. So close was the dog to Penn when the shot fired that the burning powder stung its face. It jerked back, rolling over on itself, and then shook its head to clear its burning eyes. Then it snarled again and came at him one more time.

Penn levered another round into the chamber, raised the rifle, and fired again.

This time he hit the dog, though only grazing its side. It did another flip, rolled, and ran off limping. Its snarling bark had turned to a yip of pain, and Penn dared to think that this time he'd managed to end any threat the dog presented.

A shot was fired below; a bullet sang above Penn's head, so high that he knew right away it was intended not to hit him but to warn him.

"Hold it there, nigger man!" a voice from below yelled. "Drop that rifle!"

Penn was not inclined to do either. He ran hard for the trees from which he'd crept. Another shot from below sailed over his head, but much closer. *That* shot had been intended to hit him. Penn wondered if McCutcheon could see him, and recognize him from where he was. Probably not, he thought. At this point the hillside and the remnants of the house hid him completely from the street below.

Penn plunged into the woods, cut to the right, and hid behind a tree. He then cautiously peered around.

Two men were running up the slope, passing the burned ruin and crossing the back clearing. They'd be upon him in moments.

Penn ran farther back into the woods, cursing his bad luck and that betrayer of a dog. He'd hoped to retain the advantage of not having the outlaws know he existed, but that was certainly no longer the case. They'd be on guard for him now—unless they managed to kill him here and now.

"There he is!"

Another shot, sailing through the trees, smacked into a treetop fifty feet ahead of him. Penn wheeled, raised his rifle, and fired off a quick responsive shot. He saw them fall back, then resume their running.

Penn headed up a slope and then over it, momentarily cut off from their view. The woods were ending; ahead he saw an open meadow. They'd pick him off easily. Yet he couldn't go back.

So he went to the right instead, taking advantage of the lay of the land. A small hillock rose before him, covered with brush, and he used it for cover. It led him into a small, gradually bending ravine. He followed its contour and plunged along as hard as he could. When he came out of the ravine, he found he was actually running back toward Marrowbone.

Penn entered the woods again at a different point. By now his two pursuers weren't anywhere to be seen. Either they were searching for him in the meadow, or perhaps coming through the ravine. In any case, he'd lost them for the moment, and now was the time to seal his escape.

He'd moved through the evergreen grove only a short way before he unexpectedly entered another clearing. It seemed to be the remains of a long-abandoned claim; in the midst of it was a broken-down hovel of a cabin, weathering away.

Instantly he thought of hiding in it, but gave up that idea when he realized that such a hiding place was too obvious. But he had to hide somewhere; running alone would bring him nothing better than the fate of unfortunate Kale Mason.

He spotted a rotting wooden door near the cabin, parallel to the ground and covering what he assumed was a cistern of some sort, or maybe a well tapping into some underground spring.

If it wasn't too deep, it would be a good place to hide.

He ran over, yanked the wooden trapdoor open, and looked down into the pit below. He kicked a stone in; it clattered on dry earth just a few yards down.

That was good enough for Penn. He sat on the edge of the pit, positioned the wooden cover where he could reach it with the rifle, and dropped into the hole.

Chapter Twenty-two

Penn struck bottom hard, but kept his footing. Probing with the rifle, he scooted the cover back into place, burying himself in darkness.

He felt along the wall and discovered that the hole gave way to a recess, maybe a tunnel, directly in front of him. He realized that this was probably a mine shaft dating back to Marrowbone's first days, and covered by the wooden door for safety. How far back the tunnel went he couldn't see, but as he cautiously proceeded into it, he advanced fifteen feet before he struck a dead end. This was one mine, apparently, that had died aborning; perhaps the stony wall before him was a "horse," as miners called the great iron-ore boulders that all too frequently stopped their progress below ground. The ceiling of the tunnel was so low that Penn had to stoop, and the sense of enclosure, the dank earthen smell, and the pitch darkness made him feel terribly claustrophobic. Even so, he felt he'd made the right move in entering this pit. His followers would be unlikely to go to the trouble of actually exploring it themselves, if they even noticed it at all. For the moment, he was safe here.

He sat down in the darkness, breathing the heavy, cool air, feeling like a mole in its tunnel.

Even if he was momentarily safe, he wished this tunnel went deeper and had some exit at the other end. If by chance they did catch him in here, he'd be trapped. He had visions of them doing something terrible, like throwing burning wood into the hole and closing the top again, choking him to death in smoke. Or dropping in snakes, or kicking that vicious dog down here with him.

He remained silent, listening. He could hear them above.

Dear Lord, don't let them lift that door! Don't let them even think to look in here!

They did lift the door. Light streamed into the hole. Penn pulled back against the wall at the end of the short tunnel, and readied himself to shoot should one of the men drop in after him.

"What is it?" a voice asked.

"An old mine shaft, I think, or the start of one. I don't think it was ever finished, 'cause it ain't very deep." A stone thunked on the bottom of the pit, startling Penn all over again. "Nah. It's real shallow."

"He down there?"

"I don't see nothing. He'd not have took time to drop into a hole, anyway."

The light was blocked out again as the shaft's cover rattled back into place.

Penn led out a deep breath. He realized what had happened. They, like him, had not been able to see the actual bottom of the pit because of the angle of the sun, or see the entrance to the short tunnel leading off to the side.

Penn listened but could not hear them anymore. They'd moved on.

Even so, he was very much a prisoner here for now. They'd continue to search for him throughout the town and, when they failed to find him, would probably alert others and intensify the search. An outside witness to what was going on in old Marrowbone was something these outlaws would not accept, and the treatment they'd given McCutcheon told Penn they were taking seriously the danger of some stranger wandering in and seeing what he shouldn't.

Penn was trapped here, at best, until dark. Only then could he hope to leave without being noticed.

A terrifying thought came to him. Could he

leave at all? It was one thing to get into a hole, another to climb out again. And this hole had no ladder, no climbing pole, nothing to help him out.

With this new concern to worry over, he sat brooding in the darkness. Eventually he changed his position, moving to the area directly under the opening, where he could look up and see little splinters of daylight coming through the wooden cover. He struck a match and examined the walls of the hole, trying to figure out a way to climb out.

It wasn't going to be easy. He wasn't sure if he could do it at all.

Nora squatted in the grove of trees, her hand clasped in terror across her mouth and tears in her eyes.

What had happened out there? Where was McCutcheon? Who were the men who had appeared with weapons and taken him prisoner?

It all had to do with Denver, and the death of her husband. Maybe they believed McCutcheon had done it, and had sent men after him! But how would they have known he would be coming to this remote place?

Maybe they were looking for him because they had managed to learn he was with her. Maybe it was *she* they were really looking for.

At the moment, anything seemed possible to Nora.

She'd always been prone to follow her instincts, but right now several impulses were in conflict within her. *Run! Hide! Follow! Seek help!*

Torn, she simply stayed where she was for several minutes until at last one impulse overcame the rest: *Hide.*

She was hidden already, but not in a place she could stay for long. She needed shelter, a place she would be safe and think about what to do now.

Nora rose, turned her back to the road, and penetrated the woodland behind her.

Jim McCutcheon was utterly mystified by what was happening to him. Who were these gunmen? And why were they holding him and a dozen or so others hostage within the old Marrowbone church, a building apparently long vacant?

His fear at the beginning had been the same as Nora's: that he was being detained in connection with what had happened back in Denver. Yet that made no sense. It was highly unlikely that he and Nora would have been tracked so far, at such great effort. Zeke Washington hadn't been the kind of citizen whose murder would spark such a reaction.

Besides, the men who'd captured him surely didn't seem like lawmen. What kind of lawmen took an entire community hostage?

The situation seemed so unreal that McCutcheon couldn't resist testing it a little with a touch of levity as his captors had shoved him inside the church.

"I've heard of churches trying to increase their attendance, but this seems to be going a bit far," he said to the gunmen.

Flippancy was not welcome. One of the riflemen poked him between the shoulder blades with the muzzle of his levered Henry. "Keep your mouth shut, if you know what's good for you," he spat.

The people on the benches, mostly men, were as solemn as the guards, but fear was apparent in their eyes. They stared at the newcomer with hesitant curiosity, but said not a word.

"Sit down," one of the gunmen ordered.

"Who's this?" asked one of the guards already in the church.

"Don't know. He just came into town."

"You want to go and tell Nathan?"

"Why would I tell Nathan? It's Marcus who I answer to." The man left.

McCutcheon sat on the bench beside one of the few men in the room not significantly older than he.

A gray-haired man in front of him turned and looked him over. "I don't know who you are, young man, but you picked a bad time to come to Marrowbone."

"I think you're right, sir."

"My name's Homer Welch. I've been in Marrowbone for a long time now, but never have I seen the likes of this. God help us all. We may be seeing the end of our days before this is through."

"Just what is going on here?" McCutcheon asked.

"Old man!" one of the guards barked at Welch. "Keep turned around this way."

Welch shook his head sadly and turned away from McCutcheon.

Chapter Twenty-three

The younger man beside McCutcheon stuck out his hand, and said softly, "My name's Romeo Lewis. Call me Roe."

McCutcheon shook the man's hand. "Jim McCutcheon. What's going on here?"

"What's going on is the takeover of this sad, worn-out old mining town by none other than the infamous Parlee brothers and their cohorts."

Parlee! McCutcheon felt the color drain from his face as he thought about that morning's encounter with Joe Parlee in Lower Marrowbone.

"Not all three Parlee brothers, though," Lewis went on. "Just two. Nathan Parlee has been doing most of the strutting and talking and order-giving. Marcus, the oldest brother, is here too, but he's wounded pretty badly and laid up in one of the cabins. Has a woman with him. From what I'm hearing, it seems that Marcus and Nathan have had a falling out with brother

Joe. I gather that it was Joe who shot Marcus. Some kind of dispute over a division of money taken in a bank robbery."

"So there's a war among outlaws."

"That's right. And a smaller one between Nathan and Marcus, as best I can tell. It seems that Nathan is trying to push himself into Marcus's place of authority while Marcus is down and out."

"I hate to bear this news, but Joe Parlee ain't far behind his brothers."

"What?"

"I ran into him in Lower Marrowbone this morning. I had something of an unexpected row with him, and left him knocked cold on the street."

Welch turned his head slightly, and McCutcheon realized the old man had just overheard what had been said.

Roe Lewis was frowning, trying to decide whether he believed this story. "Well, if that's true, we may be in even a worse fix than it appears."

"You're thinking Joe might show up and have it out with his brothers?"

"Yep. With all of us here caught right in the middle."

McCutcheon said, "I truly cannot believe this is happening."

"It's been two days for me, and I can't believe it either," Lewis said. "I'd only been in this dang town for a week before that. I figured I'd find a strike that somebody had missed the first time around. I wasn't looking for any kind of trouble. Neither were any of these other folks. Most of them are old-timers, holdovers from the old days."

"Why did the Parlees pick Marrowbone?"

"Convenience and seclusion, I guess, and the fact they happened to be nearby when Marcus Parlee was wounded. It's as good a place as they could have found. Food, shelter, no law, and nobody tends to pass through much."

McCutcheon replied, "All *I* came for was to try to return a man's sister to him."

"What?"

"A woman . . . she was traveling with me, but she hid out of sight when I was taken prisoner. By the way, you haven't seen a black man around here, have you? A newcomer, probably asking around for a woman named Nora?"

"No. Would he be a miner?"

"Just a drifter. He's been looking for a sister that was taken from him long before the war. I happened to find her . . . or somebody I think is her, anyway. He'd done me a big favor, so I figured I'd do one for him in return."

"And now look what you're into. That's what

comes of trying to do something nice for somebody."

"Yep."

"If this fellow had been here, I'd probably know it. You don't come into a community this small without being seen."

"If he'd come in, it would probably have been today," McCutcheon said. "And I suppose he'd have been brought here captive just like I've been."

"Not necessarily if he's a black man. The Parlees have been known to kill black folks before, out of sheer meanness."

McCutcheon frowned at the maze of wrinkles on the back of Welch's neck. "You heard the shooting as they were pushing me through the door, I suppose."

"I did."

"There was a man outside in one of those burned-out houses. I caught a glimpse of him. He might have been a Negro, but it was hard to be sure."

"I wonder what's become of this man?"

"I don't know. I hope he made it, whoever he is."

The men fell silent for a few moments.

"What's going to happen here?" McCutcheon finally asked.

Lewis said, "Maybe they'll ride out and let us

be. Maybe they'll line us up and shoot us, just so nobody will ever know about all this. These people are serious business. They've already killed two people here, a father and a son. The father tried to resist them, and they wounded him. The son ran away, trying to get help for his father. A couple of the Parlees' men went after him. They say they gunned him down in cold blood. But they have been feeding us the last couple of days. Not much, but enough. Why would they feed people they're planning to shoot?"

"You two, shut up that whispering!" one of the guards ordered.

They did.

Jake Penn, peering up through the little cracks in the cover of the pit, had watched the last light fade away an hour before. But still he'd stayed put, not willing to leave his hiding place until he was certain that all daylight was gone, and all searching for him in the area had ceased.

Now, he believed, it was finally safe to try. He stood, struck another match, and studied the walls around him. They were more earthen than rocky; handholds were few, and not particularly secure.

He measured the size of the opening with his arms and tried to figure the best way to climb out. Various attempts brought him nothing but short climbs, hard falls, and many bruises.

Finally, he tried bracing his back against one side of the shaft and pressing his feet against the far side. He was able to hold himself aloft in this manner, and by using his hands, he found he could claw his way upward. It was slow and straining, but it worked.

The only problem was that he couldn't carry his rifle up at the same time. It took both hands just to keep himself ascending.

He solved the problem by tearing some cloth strips from inside his coat, tying them together, then tying one end of the makeshift cord to the trigger guard of his Winchester. He tied the other end around his belt, and made sure his pistol was firmly tied down in its holster so that he wouldn't lose it while he climbed.

Penn began to ascend slowly, working very hard. It made him realize how hungry and tired he was, even though he'd done nothing but sit down in this hole most of the day. Knowing the danger that waited in the world beyond was stress enough to make him weary.

He finally reached the top of the shaft and pushed the cover off. A starlit sky appeared above him, seeming unusually bright because his eyes had adjusted so fully to the velvet-black darkness inside the hole.

Penn hooked his elbows around the sides of the pit opening and hoisted himself up and out, rolling to one side. He pulled his rifle up and untied the cord.

Placing the cover back over the shaft opening, he worked his way back to the burned-out house and hid himself there, wanting to study the lay of the town for a while before deciding what to do next.

He saw light in the windows of various cabins and huts around Marrowbone, though most were dark. There was light in the church house as well. All the people of Marrowbone were still being kept prisoner, he guessed, McCutcheon probably still among them.

What could he do to help these people? He thought again about seeking out the law, but still feared that this would result only in confrontation and the use of the townsfolk as hostages. From what he'd heard of the Parlees, and considering how readily they'd killed that young Mason boy and his father, he was sure that such a standoff would only get a lot of innocent people killed.

What Penn needed was an ally. Someone to help him plan and execute a rescue.

There was no evidence that a search for him was still underway. Maybe they'd assumed he'd gotten away, or simply decided that a search at night was hopeless. He doubted they'd completely forgotten him, though, considering how determined they'd been to get him earlier on, and how quickly McCutcheon had been roped in when they showed up.

Penn's stomach growled. He was finding it difficult to think clearly. He badly needed food. Once nourished, he could ponder over this situation much better.

He looked at the sprawling St. John house. Not a bit of light shone out, of course, given the lack of doors and windows. Maybe St. John and his surviving son were among the prisoners up in the church.

Penn noticed an interesting thing about the place: there were old heaps of dirt all around. Miniature hills that seemed difficult to account for, until Penn remembered Tennison's mention of the network of tunnels beneath the place.

Penn decided to try to find a way into the St. John house. Inside he'd probably find food, and with no exterior openings, he'd be safe from detection from the outside even if he burned a light.

He slowly worked his way across town, staying hidden, seeing no gunmen and drawing no attention. He wondered how he'd find the entrances to the tunnels leading into the St. John house. How long were those tunnels, anyway?

If they extended far enough, the entrances could be miles from the house.

Suddenly, Penn heard movement and voices.

Two men were approaching, already very near.

Chapter Twenty-four

Penn froze for a moment, uncertain what to do, then threw himself down behind a woodpile at one corner of the St. John house.

". . . and this nigger has apparently gotten away free and clear," one of the men was saying. "He just vanished, they said. Like the ground had swallowed him."

Indeed it had, Penn thought, rather proudly.

The other man said, "What if he goes and tells some lawman we're here?"

"That's what Nathan's worried will happen," the first man replied. "Either that, or Joe will get wind of where we are. Either could put us all in a bad fix."

"Who was that other fellow they caught today?"

"Just some drifter. How long do you think we'll have to hole up here?"

"Until Marcus is healed up enough to ride, I reckon."

"That could be three weeks, maybe more."

"I know. And word's bound to get out that we're here. Then the law could jump right on us."

"We ought to line up every damn one of them people in that church and shoot them. Dead men don't run or talk."

"Nathan's ready to do it. But Marcus says no."

"Nathan won't listen to him forever."

"I know. I don't much like Nathan . . . never have. But this is one time I think he's in the right. We need to rid ourselves of them people. They're dangerous to us."

"Whichever brother wins out in that argument, I ain't going to follow Nathan. Not far, anyway. He's too stupid, too full of himself, and he ain't got the smarts his brothers do. I'm for Marcus, and if he dies, then I'm out. I'll not ride with Nathan alone."

"Same for me."

They began to walk away, one digging his tobacco pouch out of his pocket.

Penn never knew quite what happened. Maybe he moved without realizing it, maybe his balance tilted a little. Whatever the cause, a stick that up until then had been resting quite easily beneath his heel decided to snap loudly. He winced.

"You hear that?" one of the men said.

"Yeah," the other whispered. "Maybe it's that nigger. Let's take a look."

Penn heard them approach, and knew he'd be caught if he didn't move quickly.

He ran at a crouch around one of the many corners of the St. John house. But they heard him, and perhaps saw a flash of him in the darkness.

"It's him, sure 'nough!" one of the men declared. "Get him, Jesse! Don't let him get away!"

Penn pounded across the weedy back lot behind the St. John house, running toward a grove of woods.

Abruptly, the ground beneath him gave way. Penn tumbled down, and as he fell, wondered if he'd run into yet another old mine shaft, this one much deeper than the one in which he'd hidden.

He struck the ground quickly, however, and saw that he wasn't in any kind of hole at all. He'd unwittingly run up the sloped, earthen roof of some sort of root cellar or other sod-covered shelter, built right into the hillside. He'd fallen into a cut-out space in front of the cellar door.

He stood quickly, yanked open the cellar

door, darted inside, and closed it behind him. He put his eye to a knothole and looked out.

As he'd hoped, his two pursuers had not seen where he had gone. Thus they passed right by the door with their backs to it, never even noticing its existence.

With his eye still pressed to the knothole, Penn grinned as he watched the men disappear into the night.

Penn stayed put for the moment, figuring they'd probably run for a good while before realizing he wasn't ahead of them.

Curiosity whispered at him, as well as suspicion. He took a matchbox with a built-in candle from his pocket. Striking a match, he touched it to the little candle and looked around.

It did look like he was in a typical root cellar. Yet it seemed odd to him that a cellar had been built this far away from any dwelling, considering that most people liked to have them right beside their houses.

Rough shelves lined the walls on both sides, but the back was simply paneled up with boards. A few crates were stacked against it, as well as some lumber. Penn walked closer and examined the back wall. As he felt along it, he noticed something and moved the candle closer.

"Ah, yes," he whispered. "So I thought."

There was a small, stick-like protrusion half-way down the wall, hardly noticeable. He lifted it; nothing happened. Pushing it down resulted in the same thing. He pushed in.

The rear wall swung open like a door. The sudden draft of wind extinguished his candle.

Penn stood there a moment trying to adjust his eyes. Cool air, dank and musty, rushed back against him. He smelled a burning, oily scent.

Penn lit another match and fired up the candle. He stepped forward cautiously, entering the black space before him.

Closing the false wall behind him, he looked around and noticed an extinguished torch at his feet, the source of the oily smell. He picked it up and relighted it, then shook out the candle and pocketed it along with the matches.

"Well, Jake, old fellow," he said to himself, "let's take a walk through Mr. St. John's tunnel."

Jake Penn had to crouch slightly to proceed along the tunnel. It was a rough tunnel, not particularly smooth on any side, but it was shored up and showed no evidence that it was in any way precarious.

As Penn walked farther back the tunnel began to turn slightly. The farther he went, the more squared-off the tunnel became, and the greater care was evidenced in its framing and shaping.

Penn paused, sniffing the air. He made a face, smelling something deeply offensive.

It was as if he'd walked into a tomb.

As he walked on, the smell grew stronger. He thought of turning back, but his curiosity drew him on. He pulled a bandana from his pocket and tied it around his face, filtering out the rancid air.

He soon encountered a door leading off the tunnel to the right. The smell was most powerful here.

Penn stood there, flickering torch in hand, black and oily smoke trailing from its flame and hugging the ceiling of the tunnel.

The door had no lock, but on its front were carved three letters that made Penn reluctant to open it. "R.I.P. ," he read beneath his breath.

But he couldn't resist. He had to know.

Penn pulled in a lungful of air through the bandana and opened the door.

The stench was overwhelming even though he was holding his breath. Flies swarmed by the hundreds.

Torchlight played over two corpses, laid out side by side. One, apparently dead much longer, was that of an old man. On his chest, clutched in his hands, were a fiddle and bow.

The other corpse, the one emanating the worst stench and the most flies, was the maggot-ridden remains of a much younger man.

Penn closed the door quickly and staggered back the way he'd come, where the air was nominally fresher. He breathed gratefully, and tried to shake off his reaction to what he'd seen.

"Mr. St. John," he said aloud, "I think old Tennison was wrong about one thing, at least. I don't believe you're alive any longer after all."

As for the second, younger corpse, Penn supposed it had to be the St. John son who had died.

So there could only be one of the St. John family remaining alive. It seemed likely that either he'd moved on, or was among the captives up at the church.

When Penn's nerves had settled a bit, he headed back up the tunnel again, hurriedly passing the door that separated him from the dead men.

Just ahead the tunnel made a sharp veer to the left. Penn looked around the corner, seeing another heavy door flickering in the torchlight.

He lightly touched the latch and found it locked. He cursed his luck, but when he gave the latch a slightly harder jiggle in frustration he found it wasn't locked after all, only slightly stuck.

He lifted the latch and pulled back on the door. It opened on well-oiled hinges with not so much as a creak or whisper.

The torch flared and danced, casting a feeble light some yards inside the emptiness, but revealing nothing but empty space.

Penn stepped through the door.

Chapter Twenty-five

Penn looked from side to side. He was in a chamber walled with stones. The ceiling above was rock and dirt, shored in place by wood timbers.

He was still underground, obviously. Did this room have an exit? he wondered. A stairway to something above?

Penn began to explore. The room was larger than he'd anticipated. The big cellar was empty except for scraps from the shoring timbers, an old barrow with the wheels gone, and assorted rusted mining tools.

Something else was ahead. He walked over and held the torch low to the ground.

Dozens of envelopes, all of them sealed, littered the floor of the cellar. He reached down, picked one up and examined it, then others. They were all addressed to Edna St. John in Chicago. There were no postmarks and therefore no way he could figure out the dates of when the letters were written, but most seemed to be several years old, if the state of the paper was an indication. All had their addresses neatly inscribed by the same careful hand. There was no return address, front or back, on any that Penn picked up.

Penn wasn't a spookish man, but this place was beginning to nag at his nerves a little. It reminded him of a place he'd visited once, a public amusement house, where the floors and walls were all tilted in odd ways, sometimes undetectably, but with startling results. Balls would seem to roll uphill rather than down. Water would flow in the opposite way it seemed it should.

It was an unsettling place to be. So was this.

The torch flickered, the flame pulling and stretching, then resettling.

Air had moved. Somewhere, some door or window or trapdoor had opened and then closed again.

Penn was glad he still had his rifle and pistol. He held the torch high, looking around and listening. He heard only the hiss of the torch flame and the scampering of a mouse across the floor.

Penn advanced. Another passage led off the other side of the chamber. He entered it, and felt the ground sloping up beneath him. Just when it grew too steep to climb easily, a rough stair-case began.

Penn walked up the stairs until he reached another door. There was wood framing the door and the walls around him now; he'd obviously reached the ground floor of the house.

There'd been a working latch once, but it was now broken. He touched the door. It swung open, creaking slightly.

The interior of the house was almost as dark as a cave, having no windows. Penn used the torch to light his way.

Furnishings were sparse, consisting of only a chair and a small table, on which sat a broken lamp.

Penn walked across the room and entered an-other. All was the same. A bit of furniture, all of it old and battered, dirt on the floor, litter, garbage . . . and footprints in the dust. He knelt and looked at them closer.

Something splashed on him; the torch went out, hissing.

Someone had doused it with a splash of water.

Startled, Penn stood too fast and tripped over his own feet. He fell, dropping his rifle and landing on his side.

Someone was there in the darkness, just above him, looming.

Penn groped for his pistol.

*   *   *

"No light!" a whispery, coarse voice said. "No light in this house! The ones on the outside will see!"

Penn got the pistol out and pointed it up at the unseen person. "Who are you?"

"I'm Fitz St. John. I live here. Who are you, and why are you in my house?"

Penn scrambled back on his rear, then rose. He reached down, found his rifle, and pulled it to him.

"I've got weapons," he said. "Don't you try anything."

"Oh, my God . . . are you one of *them*? One of those outlaws?" the disembodied voice became panicky and tight. "Please, please don't shoot me!" St. John wheezed.

"I'm not one of the outlaws. I'm a newcomer to this town, and they've tried twice to kill or catch me since I've got here. There's folks being held hostage up in the church, and all I'm trying to do is find a way to get them out."

"You won't shoot me?"

"No. Not unless you try to hurt me first. Why'd you throw water on me?"

"I had to put the torch out! They might see the light."

"There's no windows."

"But there might be knotholes and cracks in

the walls. They'd be able to see, and then they'd know someone is here."

"You nearly scared me to death!"

"What about me? I'm the one who had his house broken into!"

"Look, is there no place in here where we can have some light? I don't like talking to someone I can't see."

"You promise you won't try to hurt me?"

Tennison had said he thought it was the "loco" St. John son who had died. He was beginning to wonder if Tennison had been wrong about that. "I promise. All I came in for was a place to hide from the men chasing me, and the hope of finding something to eat. I'm nigh starved."

"Your voice sounds like a Negro's."

"It's because I am one. That bother you?"

Suddenly, St. John's voice sounded eager. "Oh, no. Not at all. I don't get to see many Negroes. Come this way—there's a place we can go where we can have light."

"Where we going? Back down in that cellar?"

"Oh, no. I hate it down there. I never go down there."

Penn paused. "Then who buried them, Fitz?"

"You saw them?" Fitz asked hesitantly.

"I did. I wasn't trying to intrude into anything

private . . . I just had to know what was in there."

"My father died first. My brother, Gerald, buried him, and laid his fiddle across his chest. And later, when Gerald got sick—he had awful tumors—he made me promise to lay him there beside Papa when he was gone. So I did. It was hard for me to do, the hardest thing I'd ever done, because I didn't want to see Papa dead, and decaying . . . but I did it. For Gerald."

Fitz was walking as he talked; Penn followed his receding footsteps. A door opened ahead. Penn was vaguely aware of a ripple on the black surface of the darkness, the faintest hint of an image of Fitz passing through the doorway.

Penn followed him through. Fitz brushed against him, closing the door behind him, then passed by again, moving through the darkness without hesitation.

A match flared suddenly and touched a candlewick, giving Penn his first look at his unusual companion.

Chapter Twenty-six

Fitz St. John was a large fellow, unusually so, with rounded shoulders, a rotund belly, and short legs that were as thick as tree trunks, vanishing into short-topped boots.

His trousers were cut wide, and his shirt was something much like an old hunter's frock, worn loose around his big body and hanging nearly to his somewhat bowed knees. His hair was quite long, nearly to his shoulders. His whiskers were long and unshaven, but wispy; his beard was like a thin, dark cloud around the base of his wide face.

Fitz might have been twenty years old, maybe thirty. His looks were so different from that of most people Penn had ever known, his skin so untouched by sun, that it was hard to judge his age. Fitz's dark eyes were the largest Penn had ever seen.

The pair looked each other over, up and

down. Then Penn noticed the walls of the room they'd entered. They were hung with layers of blankets.

"Why the blankets?" Penn asked.

"Too keep the light in, so no one will know. You really *are* a Negro. Fascinating!" Fitz stared at him with blatant interest.

"You did all this since those outlaws came in?" Penn asked, waving toward the blankets.

"Oh, no. It's been like this a long time. I don't want anyone to know I'm here. They think the house is empty, you know. Except for the ghosts. That's why they don't come, because they believe it's a haunted house. But there aren't any ghosts. Just me, here alone. Tell me: does dark skin feel different on you than white skin does?"

Penn didn't understand this man, but one thing did seem clear: Tennison's talk of madness in the St. John family was surely on the mark.

"I've never had white skin, so I can't know. I doubt it does."

"It seems to me it would, somehow. It would feel . . . *darker*." Fitz chuckled, a spastic noise.

Fitz's face suddenly did an odd thing. It seemed to squeeze suddenly, his eyes pinching shut, his mouth puckering. Penn was startled, then remembered a boy he'd known in early childhood who'd had similar sort of tic. *Just pay no attention*, Penn's mother had told him. *He can't help it.*

"So," Fitz said, "who are you?"

"I'm Jake Penn. Just a drifter . . . just a drifter who's hungry and alone, and who has a whole churchful of people he needs to get freed from some very bad men."

"Yes. Yes, I know what's happened."

"How can you know, if you stay in here?"

"I have places I can watch from. I have lofts above, with holes in the walls and little covers that slide up and down. When I look through them, I see many things that happen in Marrowbone. I see people come by here and point and talk about his place, afraid of it. They believe there's ghosts. They throw rocks sometimes. But they never, never come in. They're afraid of the tunnels." He paused. "But you weren't. Why did you come?"

"There was something much more frightening outside the tunnel than anything I figured I was likely to encounter inside it. Men with guns, wanting me caught, or dead."

"I've seen these men. I watched them take over this town. It's awful. I saw them shoot a man who was defying them, too. And I watched that man die later, out on the street, with his head on his wife's lap. I felt very sorry for her."

"Do you know who these people are, Fitz?"

"No."

"Have you ever heard of the Parlees?"

"No."

"They're outlaws. Very bad men. Three of them, brothers. One is separated from the others, fighting with them, apparently. The other two are here, but one is wounded. I was able to learn some of this from a young man a couple of the Parlees' men wounded outside town, and from overhearing conversation."

"Would they kill me if they found me?"

"They'd probably take you away and make you stay with the others in the church up on the hill."

"Oh, no. No. I'd die first. I never, *never* leave here. I never go out there."

Penn's stomach grumbled loudly. "Then how do you eat?"

"There's a man who brings food in on a wagon once a month. He'd leave the food in one of our tunnels, and we'd leave him money. Gerald made the arrangements; Gerald would go out. He wasn't like me. He wasn't afraid."

"But Gerald's dead now."

"Yes. So I have to leave the money and bring in the food myself. It's the closest I come to going outside."

"You have enough money to keep paying for this food?"

"Yes. For a time."

"And then what?"

The facial spasm that came upon the heels of that question was so intense it seemed to hurt Fitz. Penn had never seen so violent a tic. "After that . . . after that . . . after that . . ." Fitz repeated it like a litany, over and over, a dozen times or more. And Penn realized that Fitz didn't know what would happen after the money was gone.

Fitz's words faltered away.

"I'm hungry," Penn said.

Fitz didn't respond to the statement. "They said my father was a madman, you know. And I think he was."

"Why's that?"

"Well, he did the oddest things. He'd go outside and play his fiddle to punish the men who'd cheated him. He said the music made them hurt."

"Maybe it did."

"When they were gone, he burned down their houses."

"I see."

"He did other things, too. My mother's dead. But he wrote her letters. He'd write them and seal them up and address them, and then just toss them away."

"In the cellar."

"Yes. How did you know?"

"I found them."

"Oh. Right." Fitz paused. "It must be interesting to have such dark skin. By the way, I think I'm probably mad, too. I hope that doesn't frighten you."

"No, of course not." *Not that I wouldn't sleep with one eye open if you were close by.*

"I'm harmless, you see. I'd never hurt anyone. I don't even have any weapons in the house . . . and I wish you hadn't brought the ones you have."

Don't expect me to surrender them, Penn thought. "These are my tools by which I defend myself against the bad men outside."

"Don't worry. I won't take them. Just don't make me touch them."

Penn was disappointed to hear of the lack of weaponry inside the house. He'd hoped to arm himself better, and replenish his ammunition supply here.

"Can I have some food?" he asked.

"Oh, certainly. I have good food. I'll bring you something. Do you like meat, bread?"

Penn, fearing that the meat served here might be fresh rat or boiled mouse, decided that this was an occasion upon which man could indeed live by bread alone. "Just a good loaf would suit me," he said.

Fitz St. John shuffled out of the room, opening and closing the door very quickly to minimize spillage of light. Penn stood alone, looking around and marveling at this bizarre, hidden world he'd uncovered. Unusual as it was, it was probably the safest place he could be in Marrowbone at the moment.

Penn wondered if people really did think of this place as haunted. It wouldn't take a hard stretch of the imagination to think so. Penn wondered, though, if the real reason people left the place alone was simply because they thought it was unoccupied, that all the St. Johns were dead and gone. With Fitz living in darkness, striking no lights except in a blanket-sealed room, and never leaving the place, it was quite possible that the other residents of Marrowbone didn't even know he was still here.

Chapter Twenty-seven

St. John returned with bread and water, and also, to Penn's pleasant surprise, a wedge of excellent cheese.

Penn gratefully devoured the food; it seemed to please Fritz St. John to watch him eat.

Then Fitz grew thoughtful, and rather melancholy. He said, "I suppose that when the money is gone, I'll either have to learn to mine gold or maybe just kill myself."

"Don't you talk about killing yourself. You don't want to do that," Penn said, chewing a hunk of bread.

"I can't go out, though."

"Sure you can. It's easy. When all this is over, I'll help you do it. You'll see."

"No, no. Not me."

"We'll talk about it later." Penn took a bite of cheese. "Mine gold, did you say?"

"Yes. That's where Papa and Gerald got the

means to pay for things. Papa found a little strike of gold in one of the tunnels. He mined it as long as he could, and then Gerald took over for him. Now all I have left is what they dug out."

"If you've got a gold strike, you need to make the best of it. Learn to mine it, then get out of this place and live a regular kind of life. You'd like it. It's fun, living life to its fullest."

"I like being alone. I like the dark."

"Yes, but the dark is like a prison. It keeps you from being free. And a man ought to be free if he can. I was a slave when I was a boy, but I ran away and got myself free. And free's better than slavery, I can tell you."

Fitz thought about it. "Do you want more food?"

"No. No, that was just right. Later, maybe, I'll have more. And I'll pay you for it, soon as I can."

"All I ask is that you let me touch your skin."

"Huh?"

"I want to see what such dark skin feels like."

Penn felt odd doing it, but he pulled up a sleeve and extended his arm. Fitz touched it, looking at it closely and rubbing it curiously. He pulled his hand away and nodded. "It feels dark, too."

Madness, indeed. Penn hoped the fellow really was harmless, like he said.

"Fitz, I'm a man with a problem."

"What's that?"

"There's a church full of innocent folks up on the hill, and I've got to find a way to get them free before something bad happens."

"But how?"

"Are you sure there's no weapons here at all?"

"No. I took them all apart and buried them after Papa and Gerald died."

"And no bullets?"

"No. There's nothing here like that at all."

"I see."

"Except for Papa's dynamite."

Penn cocked his head. "What'd you say?"

"There's Papa's dynamite. I didn't do anything with it, because I'm afraid of it."

"Where is it?"

"In a room off one of the tunnels, the one leading to the mine."

"How many tunnels are there?"

"Three. But you don't want the dynamite, do you? It's dangerous."

Penn mulled it over. "I may need something dangerous, Fitz. It might be the only tool I have to change the situation for the people in that church house. Tell me: are there detonators? Fuses?"

"Yes."

"All safely stored?"

"All locked away in boxes with straw. I never touch it . . . I'm afraid it will blow up."

"It's old dynamite?"

"Yes. Very, very deadly."

"Will you show me where it is? I'd like to look at it."

Fitz frowned, thinking. "Very well. Just don't make me go near it."

"I won't. I promise."

The old man's name was Clarence Gregg. He'd been in Marrowbone for almost a decade, having come as a miner with his son. An accident had taken his son's life, and Gregg had continued on alone, never successful enough to be truly comfortable, but never unsuccessful enough to justify throwing aside his mining tools and giving up altogether.

He arose from his place on the church house bench, and slowly walked toward one of the guards. He was one of the few gunmen whom McCutcheon had heard called by name: Eebeck.

McCutcheon, who'd been sitting there wondering if Nora was still hiding in that same grove of trees outside town, watched Gregg advance toward Eebeck.

"Sit down, old man," Eebeck said. "Nobody said you could get up."

"Please, sir, but I need to be excused to the privy."

That brought a general muttering among the prisoners, most of whom felt the same need, but had been reluctant to bring it up. Over the past two days, they'd learned that the request was inevitably treated by the guards as quite troublesome and annoying.

"Aw, hell," Eebeck muttered. "Just hold it, old man."

"I can't. You can send somebody to guard me while I do. Maybe these other people can also be allowed to go, too? It's been hours. Show some human kindness, for God's sake."

An assenting murmur swept the little crowd.

"Go sit down."

"Please sir . . . please. I really do need to go. I'm getting old, you see. I have . . . difficulty with such things."

McCutcheon pitied the old man, who was obviously embarrassed at having to plead about such personal details before a crowd of people.

"That's a shame. Do you have difficulty sitting down and shutting up, too?"

"*Please*, sir, I'm begging you."

"And I'm telling you to get the hell away from me, sit down, and shut your damn mouth."

The old man shuddered suddenly, and whispered, "Oh, no."

Eebeck looked down in disgust at the pool forming at the old fellow's feet. Gregg's trousers were soaked, his socks and boots as well. An acrid smell filled the church house.

"I'm sorry," Gregg said, tears welling in his eyes. "I'm so very sorry. I couldn't help it, I really couldn't." He turned to the other people. "I'm so very sorry."

Eebeck swore and knocked the aging man down with a rifle butt against his forehead.

McCutcheon was so stunned to see this brutality that he simply froze, paralyzed with fury.

Beside him, though, Roe Lewis was not paralyzed at all. The frustrations and anger associated with this imprisonment boiled over abruptly, and he rose with an enraged yell and charged straight at Eebeck.

Eebeck hadn't been expecting this, and didn't have time to raise his rifle before Lewis was upon him. Lewis grabbed the outlaw around the neck, choking him, yelling furiously in his face.

Clarence Gregg, sodden and humiliated, struggled to his feet and staggered back to his bench, still muttering, "I'm sorry . . . I'm sorry," gripping his injured forehead.

In the crowd, Ginny Mason rose and shouted jubilant support for the man choking the villain who'd helped kill her son.

It was hopeless, though. In seconds another guard pulled Lewis off Eebeck, who staggered away rubbing his neck, his face turned crimson.

Lewis managed to get his hand on the butt of the second guard's pistol, but was unable to yank it free because it was strapped in the holster.

Eebeck came back into action. He approached the struggling pair, and clubbed Lewis to the ground with the butt of his rifle.

Lewis lay there, stunned, while Eebeck took aim at his forehead at point-blank range.

"Hold on there, Eebeck!"

The voice bellowed from the rear of the room and brought a halt to everything going on. Eebeck looked up; the horrified prisoners turned their heads.

Nathan Parlee stalked in through the door and up to the front of the congregation. He looked down at the stunned, blank-eyed Lewis.

"What are you doing? Were you about to shoot this man?"

"I was, Nathan. He jumped me."

Nathan sniffed the air, frowning. "Smells like piss in here!"

"One of the old coots on that bench yonder peed in his britches."

"Hell, aren't you letting these people visit the privy every now and again?"

"Let 'em hold it, I say. It's a lot of trouble to herd them out, then herd them back in."

"Folks got to do these things, Eebeck. Law of nature." Nathan turned and snapped his fingers at the other guards. "Take these folks out in a straight line, and give them a chance to do what they need to do. Then bring them right back."

Eebeck pointed his rifle at Lewis. "What about him?"

McCutcheon rose from his seat. "Please, sir, let me speak. I hope you'll spare that man. He was angry because Mr. Eebeck there struck an old man with his rifle."

"You did that, did you, Eebeck?"

"He'd just peed on the floor right before me, Nathan. Smell so strong it made me sick."

"Well, maybe he couldn't help it."

McCutcheon sat down, wondering if the infamous Nathan Parlee had at least some human decency about him, and maybe wasn't as hard a man as his reputation allowed.

"We can't let these people get to thinking they can jump us and get away with it, Nathan,"

Eebeck said. "No matter what reason they do it for."

Nathan Parlee rubbed his chin. The townsfolk were now beginning to form a line to head out the door. Two men were helping the badly staggered, dizzy Clarence Gregg keep afoot on legs that had grown weak.

"You're right, Eebeck," Nathan said. He turned to the people. "Folks! Wait just a minute before you leave. Got something here you need to see."

Nathan pulled his pistol from its holster, aimed at Lewis's head, and executed him with a single shot.

In the stunned silence that followed, Nathan Parlee said, "Now let that be a lesson to you. Hear?"

Chapter Twenty-eight

Screams erupted from the women, shouts and protests from the men. Someone made retching noises, but managed to avoid being sick, probably afraid the offense would result in a bullet.

Nathan Parlee holstered his pistol and raised his hands to quiet them.

"What you just saw happen is unpleasant, but it had to be done. Now, folks, we tried to give you a lesson today, but apparently it didn't take. You saw what happened to that fine father and son who didn't cooperate like they should. And now you've seen what happened to this ill-advised 'hero' on the floor. Does anyone else need further demonstration of the fact that lack of cooperation with us simply ain't going to pay?"

Ginny Mason swooned and fainted. Ada Westmoreland, a younger woman who'd come to Marrowbone only a month earlier with her husband, went to her side and began to tend her.

"Don't nobody try to run while you're out there," Nathan said. "Don't nobody attack one of your guards. Don't be stupid. You understand? Otherwise, you get what those fool Masons got, and what this fellow got . . . what was his name, anyway?"

"He was Romeo Lewis, a better man on his worst day than you'd be after a thousand baptisms, you murdering son of a bitch!" shouted Sherman Booker, another miner.

"Romeo, huh?" Nathan laughed. He nudged the dead man with his boot toe. "Wherefore art thou *now*, Romeo?" he said, and laughed again.

McCutcheon wanted to kill him. He played with a fantasy of somehow getting his hands on Eebeck's Winchester rifle and blasting away, shot after shot, until every one of the outlaws lay dead. Except Nathan. He'd not die by a bullet, but slowly and in excruciating pain. But as it was, all McCutcheon could do was stand watching, helpless and frustrated.

Homer Welch spoke up, his voice quaking in anger. "Tell me something, outlaw: what kind of terms are you on with your two brothers right now?"

"Who the hell are you, and what makes you think you can go asking me questions?"

"My name's Welch. Homer Welch. And I'm making it my affair. The way I hear it, you and your brother Marcus have had a falling out with your other brother. I hear it was Joe who shot Marcus. Is that right?"

"Shut up and go take your leak, you cur."

"I got news for you, Nathan Parlee. Your brother Joe is right on your tail. He was seen in Lower Marrowbone just this morning. He's coming to clean you out of here, bet you anything you want to bet!"

McCutcheon closed his eyes and shook his head. He'd not wanted this news to get out.

Nathan stomped straight over to Welch and shoved his menacing face into Welch's. "Where did you hear that?"

Welch, looking into Nathan's intense eyes, suddenly lost some of his fire. "I overheard somebody say it, that's all."

"Who?"

"Him, over there." He pointed at McCutcheon. Nathan spun and faced him.

"What's your name?"

"Alexander the Great."

Nathan whipped out his pistol and jammed it under McCutcheon's chin. "Best answer me straight right now, or die!"

"My name's Jim McCutcheon."

"Is it true, what the old man said?"

Odd, McCutcheon thought. *His voice is different. Nathan Parlee is afraid . . . afraid of his own brother.*

McCutcheon had no idea what might happen now that the two Parlees learned that their estranged brother was close by. The situation was already too unpredictable, too volatile to throw new kinks into the plow line. Nathan Parlee might just decide to gun down the lot of them and haul himself out of Marrowbone to avoid any unwanted encounters with his brother Joe, especially if he was as scared of him as he seemed to be.

So McCutcheon simply denied he knew anything. "I don't know what the gentleman thinks he heard, but I didn't see your brother today or any other day. I wouldn't know the man if I laid eyes on him."

Welch was angered by this. "He's lying!" he declared. "I heard him talking about it to that young man you just killed. I was sitting right in front of him, heard every word! He said he and Joe Parlee had words, and that he knocked him out!"

"You knocked out *Joe*?" Nathan asked.

"I told you, I didn't even see Joe," McCutcheon said.

Nathan stared into his eyes. McCutcheon didn't falter or blink. Nathan wheeled and barked out to the guards: "Go ahead and get these people to the privy. Let's get it done."

McCutcheon started to join the line. "All but you," he said. "You ain't going nowhere until I'm satisfied you're telling me the truth. Roland, you stay in here and watch him. Don't let him go piss, don't let him have no food, and don't let him lie down to sleep. This one sits right there, without rising, until I say otherwise. If he's seen Joe, I intend to know about it."

Another gunman came through the door. "Nathan," he said. "Marcus is calling for you."

"I'm busy at the moment."

"He says it's important. He said he wants you to come now."

Nathan swore loudly. "Keep an eye on him," he said to one of the other guards. "I'll be back as soon as I see what the hell it is that Marcus wants."

One of the guards, a stocky man with a sawed-off shotgun, nodded his acceptance of Nathan's order, and gruffly directed McCutcheon to his seat.

McCutcheon sat down, closed his eyes, and wondered what Jake Penn would do in such a situation.

One thing he was sure of: Penn wouldn't just

sit here, a pawn ready to be knocked off the board.

Penn. He hoped that had been him in the burned-out house. Maybe he was out there even now, coming up with some kind of plan.

Wouldn't it be something if Jake Penn rescued me again! he thought. *But I can't take the chance of waiting on him. This time it's got to be me who helps myself.*

He eyed the guard, and the shotgun he held, his mind turning.

The tunnel into which Fitz led Penn was a different one than the one through which Penn had entered. This one led off a room in a different section of the house, and did not access the cellar room. An uneven, hewn flight of stairs led straight down from the main level of the house into a tunnel that was narrower, but taller, than the first one Penn had explored.

Ahead of Penn, the big, slump-shouldered form of Fitz St. John moved like a giant shadow, holding a torch that sent oily smoke toward the top of the passage.

"This is the longest tunnel," Fitz said, talking loudly so that Penn, behind him, could hear. "That's the reason that Papa chose it as the one where we should put the dynamite room. He and Gerald carved the room out. I even helped some."

"Is this dynamite still usable?"

"I don't know. I suppose it is. Does it get where it won't work if it gets old?"

"I don't know much about dynamite, but I think I've heard it actually grows more dangerous with age."

"Oh! Then we must be very, very careful."

"I intend to be."

The tunnel made a long, left curve. Penn felt fresh air against his face, blowing in from a still-unseen opening to the outside world. The breeze prompted him to ask a question.

"Fitz, does this tunnel have a door at its far end?"

"No. The end of this one is open, but the entrance is well hidden. It's the same tunnel where food is stored, too."

"Nobody's ever tried to enter your house this way?"

"Nobody's ever found the tunnel entrance, that I know of."

"With all the food stocked up there, you're fortunate no bear took up residence in here."

That stopped Fitz in his tracks. "We never thought of that. Do you think there may be bears now?"

"I doubt it. Forget I said anything."

A few paces on, Fitz stopped again. "There's the door," he said, waving the torch toward an obviously homemade door very similar to the one that had barred the tomb room off from the other tunnel. "The dynamite's in there. That door hasn't been opened for years."

"It'll be opened now. I have to find some kind of weapon to use against these outlaws."

"How will you see? Do you want my torch?"

"Not inside that room, not with all those explosives. You stand back in the tunnel and let a little light in. But for heaven's sake, don't get the flame near the dynamite."

Fitz had turned in Penn's direction. His face was contorting in the torchlight. "I'm afraid," he said. "I don't want to blow up."

"Then wedge the end of the torch in behind that wall timber there, and leave it. You can go back up to the house."

Fitz was glad to obey. He tried to get the torch in place quickly, but bungled the job, almost dropping the torch several times.

"I'll take care of it," Penn said, taking the torch from him.

"Thanks," Fitz said. He turned back and hurried off the way they'd come, plunging into the familiar darkness.

Penn put the torch in place; its light spilled across the unopened door.

He paused, frowning, and looked toward the end of the tunnel, still invisible around a couple of turns ahead. It seemed to him he'd heard a noise, maybe sensed a presence . . . but he waited, and saw and heard nothing more. Just the wind blowing in, or some creature scuttering through, he supposed.

Penn put his hand to the old, crude wooden latch and pulled the door open.

It creaked mightily, opening with a gust of air. Time, mildew, and mold had sealed the door closed over the years. Penn made a face at the dank smell that exuded from the room.

His own shadow, cast by the firelight, kept him from seeing what was inside. He moved slightly, spotting a series of stacked crates in the dim light.

Penn entered the room and knelt beside the nearest crate. It was nailed shut, but only lightly, and with a bit of careful prying, he was able to open the box.

Gently pushing aside the straw inside it, he saw a stack of long cylinders. Dynamite.

Chapter Twenty-nine

He stared at what he'd found, thinking about the fact that dynamite was made from nitroglycerin, and nitroglycerin tended to explode when shaken . . . didn't it? In his busy life, Penn had done many things, but dealing with explosives wasn't one of them. He'd heard, though, that the very advantage of dynamite was that, by absorbing the nitroglycerin, it made nitroglycerin more stable. So maybe he was being too worrisome here.

He cautiously reached inside and pulled out a stick. There was nothing particularly lethal-looking about it, but it did seem quite old. He wondered what he would need to set the stuff off.

Dynamite, he knew, was generally set off by some kind of detonator that itself was fired off by a fuse. He poked around in other boxes, and soon found lengths of fuse, and a supply of what he thought were detonators. He studied these, figuring out how all the pieces fit together, and soon felt sure that, if need be, he could actually make a piece of this stuff explode.

It made him nervous to handle it. But he was glad to have possession of something that might give him an advantage. Even the odds a little.

That wasn't to say, though, that he had the slightest notion of exactly what he was going to do.

He had dynamite, but no clear plan.

As he crouched, balanced on his ankles, Penn heard a noise behind him and twisted around suddenly, convinced he'd heard someone in the passage.

"Fitz? Is that you?"

No one replied.

Penn rose, walked out of the dynamite room, and took the torch from its place on the wall. He advanced through the tunnel toward its end until he saw the rounded and surprisingly low end of it, moonlight spilling in, filtered by evergreens. He went out and looked around. The tunnel indeed ended in a very hidden hollow filled with conifers and surrounded by up-sloping ground. He was in the midst of a kind of natural bowl that would be totally camouflaged unless someone happened to chance upon it.

He saw no sign of anyone else in the moonlit

hollow, and heard no telltale sounds. He was probably wrong, he decided. There'd been no one in the passage but himself. Just his nerves getting to him, that was all.

He returned to the tunnel and the little storage room, and took several sticks of dynamite and placed them in the large interior pocket of his coat. He took detonators and fuses as well, and checked his supply of matches.

Being quite careful with the torch, mindful that he carried enough explosives to disintegrate himself several dozen times over, he headed back up the tunnel toward the St. John house.

Nora waited a long time before she came out from behind the tree that had hidden her from the man who'd just emerged from the tunnel. She'd scrambled away just in time to avoid him seeing her.

She supposed she'd been foolish to remain hidden in the tunnel after the two men came, more foolish still to get so close to the door that she could see the black one as he handled the material in the boxes. But she'd been curious, and afraid that trying to run would only increase the chances they'd see her. She'd actually been dozing when the sound of the approaching men had awakened her. It had surprised her greatly, and made her realize that what she'd taken to be a mine with a single entrance was actually a mine, or at least a tunnel, that had access from some other place, deeper in.

Nora wasn't certain, but she thought that what was in the box was dynamite. She'd seen pictures before, and heard Zeke talk about it a lot. Zeke always had big fantasies of getting his hands on dynamite and using it to blow up a bank safe. He'd be a rich man after that, he always said.

Nora returned to the tunnel and entered it, letting the shadows swallow her. She'd not remain here now that she knew that others were here as well, but she would remain long enough to do something for her own safety.

She'd arm herself with some of that dynamite. Just one stick, maybe two, and some detonators and fuses. She already had matches in a pocket of her ragged skirt.

It was probably dangerous to carry dynamite around, she supposed, but surely no more dangerous than being in this place without any kind of weapon at all. She was sure that she was being sought by the law from Denver for killing Zeke. Who else would have taken McCutcheon prisoner like that?

At least with dynamite, she'd have something

she could threaten with, and protect herself
with.

She tiptoed slowly through the tunnel until
she reached the little room. The black man was
gone now. She opened the door, struck a match,
and examined the boxes. She took a couple of
dynamite sticks and hid them inside her jacket,
along with some fuses and detonators.

She shook out the match and closed the door.
Back out in the passage, she pondered what to
do next.

Nora worried about the men she'd seen. And
wondered if, by some narrow chance, the black
one might be Jake Penn. McCutcheon had certainly expected to find him in Marrowbone. But
she had no way to know.

Curiosity overwhelming her, Nora advanced
deeper into the tunnel, walking through the
dark passage by feel and sound, listening to the
gusts of her own breathing. But soon she grew
fearful, and turned to head back toward the end
of the tunnel and the open air.

Nathan Parlee walked away from the church
toward one of the larger miner cabins, which
stood on a hillside straight across from the
church building. He paused on the side of the
hill and looked across the dark little mining

town, wondering if Joe was out there with his men, watching.

It would be just like Joe to track him and Marcus down, and try to finish what he'd started when he put that bullet in his own brother. Nathan knew Joe well, and that he wouldn't hesitate to kill Marcus. Joe was convinced—rightly, as Nathan knew—that Marcus had cheated him, and Joe wasn't the kind to forget or forgive. Not even his own kin.

Nathan, as youngest of the three, was caught in the middle of his brothers' feud, and didn't like being there. Instinctively he knew that Joe was the wild card in the Parlee deck, the unpredictable, dangerous one, the one with no loyalties but to himself. In a way, Nathan admired that quality. He idolized and idealized it, fantasized about living that same way himself, and tried to when he could.

Realistically, though, he knew that he was very much bound to Marcus, the recognized leader. Marcus's domination, he knew, was what accounted for the success, size, and unusual stability of the Parlee gang. Marcus held the respect of the men who let him lead them; they followed him, for the most part, with the devotion of soldiers following a beloved military general. That was something rarely seen among the self-centered individualists who were drawn toward the criminal life, and the value of it wasn't lost on Nathan.

Nathan knew the self-centeredness of criminals well, for that trait was very much part of his own personality. And therein lay the opposite side of the coin regarding his attitude toward Marcus.

Marcus might have brought strength, loyalty, and stability to the infamous Parlee gang, but he also generated a biting jealousy in his youngest brother. Why should Marcus hold all the authority, receive all the respect? True, the men generally obeyed Nathan's orders, especially now, while Marcus was wounded and largely out of commission . . . but there was a difference in attitude toward him that Nathan could feel. He was, at the bottom of it all, forever the youngest brother, the overgrown boy, the one not to be taken quite as seriously, the one to nudge and whisper about when he wasn't looking, and to obey only because it was the most prudent thing to do under the circumstances.

As Nathan trudged up the hill toward the cabin where Marcus lay, he admitted fully to himself that a part of him hoped that Marcus would die. If the big tree was felled, he would no longer have to stand in its shadow.

Yet another part of him was terrified by that same prospect. If Marcus was gone, Nathan wasn't sure he would be able to maintain any control at all over the Parlee gunmen.

He also wasn't sure that he might not be in just as much danger from Joe as was Marcus himself.

Chapter Thirty

There were two gunmen there, watching the place. From the moment the gang had come into this town—bursting into cabins, taking hostage the population of mostly old, burned-out miners working old, worked-out claims, rounding the people up, herding them into the church—Nathan had been having more fun than he'd had all his life. Just as he'd enjoyed shooting the fool named Mason, and relished sending his two best gunmen to chase down and kill Mason's son. Nathan had never felt such a sense of power as he had in the midst of those episodes.

"I hear Marcus wants to see me," he said to the guards, acting as if this were all a very great bother.

The guards nodded him in.

He saw Rosalita first, and felt anew that familiar jealousy that Marcus always aroused in him.

Rosalita was a Mexican beauty, glittering eyes and raven hair, skin a rich, light brown, her lips full and marvelous to behold. But she was very thoroughly Marcus's, and Nathan knew the contempt in which she held him. It made him hate her even as he desired her.

"He still in there?" Nathan asked, thumbing toward the door to the only other room in the place. He felt ridiculous as soon as he'd said it. Rosalita could make him feel awkward just by looking at him with those dark, beautiful, loathing eyes.

Nathan didn't wait for her to answer him, but turned away from her toward the other room. She grasped his arm.

"He's weak. Don't upset him," she said.

"Let go of me."

Her voice was very low, so Marcus wouldn't overhear. "I mean it, Nathan. I know how you feel about him, the things you say. The men know you want Marcus gone, so you can take his place. But you will never be able to do it. The men will never follow you. They obey you now only because they know Marcus expects them to."

"I didn't come up here to talk to you," Nathan said, jerking his arm free. "Keep your greasy hands off me from now on, *señorita*."

Nathan stomped into the room where Marcus

lay, barechested and bandaged. Nathan stared down at his ailing older brother. "You wanted to see me?"

"I did. I want to know what the hell's going on out there. I've heard shooting, and Dave Pogue says there's some darky running free."

"There's one, yes. We're still looking for him. But we'll catch him."

Marcus scooted himself up in the bed a little, wincing. "You'll catch him if he's still around . . . and why would he stick around now, huh? You tell me that."

"We'll catch him, Marcus. Wait and see if we don't."

"I can't afford to wait and see. What if that darky's gone to the law? What'll we do if some posse comes riding in here? It's your job to keep this place sealed off, Nathan. You fail at it, as you already have, and you endanger every one of us."

Nathan felt his face growing red. "We've got hostages. And there's no posse out there."

"Not yet, maybe."

"So what the hell do you want me to do, Marcus?" Nathan stormed. "We tried to find that nigger. He just vanished. Twice. That's what they tell me."

"Twice?"

"That's right." A self-defensive argument fell

together at once in Nathan's mind. "He disappeared while it was still daylight. Then he
turned up again after dark. And what does that
show you, Marcus? That he didn't run off. He
could have, but he didn't. And I'll bet he's still
here, and that means we'll find him."

"You better find him. We can't deal with an
armed posse right now, Nathan. You find that
darky and keep an eye on him. Kill him if you
have to."

"Is this all you called me up here for? To tell
me to do what I'm already doing?"

"I'm telling you not to mess this thing up,
Nathan. I'm in no shape to fix your mistakes."

Nathan's eyes narrowed. Don't talk to me that
way, Marcus. I've got control of what's going
on in this town. There've been no mistakes."

"That's good. And it better be true."

Nathan stood there, torn. At the moment he
desired the guidance of the older brother that,
however reluctantly, he knew to be wiser than
he. He wanted to tell Marcus about Joe being
near . . . but knew it would make him seem too
much like the helpless younger brother.

Besides, Marcus would somehow blame him
for it. Make it out to be his fault that Joe had
tracked them down.

If he had. Nathan didn't yet know for sure.

He'd not had a chance to interrogate that newest hostage back at the church.

He decided that he would say nothing. Not yet. Perhaps the entire thing was a false scare. Or a situation that, somehow, he could use to prove himself both to Marcus and to the rest of the men.

"Marcus, I've got things to deal with, and no more time to waste here. If you don't have anything else to say to me, then I'm leaving."

"Go on. Get out of here."

"Heal up, Marcus. We can't hide out here forever."

"I just hope to hell that Joe doesn't find us."

That comment made Nathan's stomach churn, but he didn't show it. Without another word he turned and walked away, pointedly ignoring Rosalita.

He walked into the night and headed down the hill toward the church.

He had just begun to near the building when he saw them coming toward him at a dead run.

Jake Penn prepared to leave the St. John house by way of the same tunnel through which he'd entered. Fitz St. John, a stranger not long before, now seemed sad to see him leave, and was concerned about him. It didn't surprise Penn. He'd spent enough time on his own in his lifetime to know that every man needs the company of others, even a frightened, mentally ill hermit who'd spent the last half of his life locked indoors in a house with no windows and no light.

"What will you do, Jake?" Fitz asked him as he left.

"I honestly don't know," Penn answered. "If you're a praying man, say one for me."

"I will," Fitz answered.

He dropped to his knees, hands clasped, even as Penn descended to the cellar. Penn found it unexpectedly touching.

He passed through the tunnel, hoping that God heard the prayers of hermits.

Jesse Lakin, who'd ridden with the Parlees for five years now, was the one who delivered the news to Nathan on the hillside.

He and two other Parlee gunmen had come running down to meet him as he'd started up the hill.

"Harley's dead," Lakin said. "He's lying up there on the floor of the church with his head smashed in from the side."

"Dead? Who the hell—"

"It was that new man, the one you made stay there while all the others went to privy. He got the jump on Harley while the others were gone. Bashed his head in with his own shotgun. Now he's gone, and he's got the shotgun, and Harley's pistol and gunbelt, too.''

Nathan swore violently.

"I suppose we ought to go ask Marcus how he wants to handle this," another gunman, Dave Pogue, said.

At that, Nathan swore even more vehemently, then said, "Don't say a word to him. Not one word. All he'd tell you is that we've got to find him before he gets away, and that ain't nothing we don't already know."

"That's two running loose now," Pogue said. "That darky, whoever he is, and this fellow."

"McCutcheon," Nathan said, suddenly remembering the name. "Jim McCutcheon. Dave, I'm giving you a task. Gather up some of the men and go out hunting. Spread across this whole sorry town. I want this McCutcheon found, and I want him brought back alive. I need to talk to him."

"What about the darky?"

"Find him, too. Then kill him."

Chapter Thirty-one

I t was time to leave.

Nora had had enough of Marrowbone to suit her. Whether or not the man she'd seen was Jake Penn didn't really matter to her now, nor did she care what became of McCutcheon. He'd been kind to her, certainly, and had done much for her at considerable risk and sacrifice to himself, but she was through with him now. If the men who'd taken him were lawmen out of Denver, he might be betraying her right now, telling them that she'd killed Zeke Jackson and informing them where they might find her.

She'd never let herself be caught. The devil could take Jim McCutcheon and Jake Penn both: Nora was going back to Lower Marrowbone, and find herself something to eat. She was nearly starved.

The dynamite she carried made her nervous, but it also gave her comfort. At least she'd have

something to protect herself with, if it came to
that. But most likely she'd encounter no dangerous situations. She'd wind her way back down
the trail in the darkness and be in Lower Marrowbone by morning.

It wasn't hard to keep to the trail, which followed Marrowbone Creek. She could probably
travel by the sound of the creek alone, if she
had to. And it might come to that; the sky had
started to grow overcast minutes ago, the moon
growing dim and the stars winking out a score
at a time. Off in the distance she heard thunder
rumble, and saw a flare of heat lightning on
the horizon.

Nora hurried her pace, eager to reach Lower
Marrowbone as soon as possible.

The moon sailed behind thickening clouds
and vanished. Nora continued on, more slowly,
missing the light the moon afforded her and
wondering if she'd be able to make it after all.

A moment later, though, the moon passed
into a break in the clouds and shone down
more brightly.

Nora stopped, suddenly terrified.

A line of figures, dark and hard to make out,
but certainly real and certainly there, loomed before her. She could not see their shadowed faces,
but felt their eyes locked on her.

She froze for a few moments, then began groping under her jacket for a stick of dynamite. One of the figures was advancing toward her.

Penn had placed his hope in a sudden burst of inspiration once he actually got out into the open town. So far, such a burst hadn't come.

But something was happening, even if not for him. There was great activity up near the church, with gunmen coming out and talking hurriedly among themselves, fanning out in different directions.

Penn hid behind a stack of firewood near an empty miner's cabin and watched. When one of the scattering hardcases began heading in his direction, he ducked low, making himself small and huddling in the shadows behind the stacked firewood. He hoped the man wouldn't come near him.

The man did, though, passing right by the stack of wood. He never noticed Penn, but he was obviously on the hunt for someone. Penn wondered if somehow he had prompted this hunt. But though he was sure they did want to see him captured, he didn't think this search had been instigated by him. The way the men had left the church, the way orders had been barked and the gunmen had spread out, spoke of a fast and desperate reaction to something that had happened up near the church. Penn couldn't guess what. Maybe one of the captives had escaped.

He had to know what was going on. When the searcher was well past him, Penn rose and darted into the shadows behind a cabin nearer to the church, then from there to yet another hiding place, working his way up the hill.

He was determined to get a look through one of those church windows, and see just how many captives there were, and how serious this situation was.

Nathan was inside the church now, looking down at Harley Jones's corpse, trying to hide his surprise and disbelief from the captives, several of whom were quite distraught at the moment. None were unhappy that one of their captors were dead, but many feared what Nathan Parlee might do to retaliate. He'd already demonstrated his propensity for cruelty and revenge, and what had been done to Jones was an act he was unlikely to let pass unanswered.

Jones's body was an ugly sight. He was sprawled out on the floor on his back, the right side of his head misshapen, clubbed inward.

"I figure this McCutcheon must have done it with Jones's own shotgun butt," Eebeck said. "He must have moved fast. Harley was well armed, and McCutcheon wasn't, and still he got the drop on him. We'd best catch him. And that darky, too, if he's still about. If a posse comes our way, we'd be in a hard situation."

Hearing a viewpoint so reflective of the harangues Nathan had already heard from Marcus only made him angry. "You think I don't know that, Eebeck? Get out of here! You're wasting time here when you could be out hunting them down. Get going!"

"Who's going to guard these people?" Eebeck asked.

"Fetch Will Lesley and Eric Grover," Nathan said. "Guarding a bunch of old folks is about all they're good for, anyway. I need you men outside hunting. And tell Lesley and Grover that if these folks give them problems, gun them down."

Many faces paled, for no one doubted he meant the order to be taken seriously.

Ginny Mason stared coldly at Nathan Parlee. He noticed, and returned the stare. Hers did not falter, and it still held when he broke away and headed out the door.

Nora backed away as the dark figure approached. She was so scared her hands fumbled numbly, unable to get hold of the dynamite under her coat. She realized, too, that even if she did get hold of it, there was no time to position the detonator and fuse, much less strike a match.

"Don't hurt me!" she said. "Please don't! I swear it wasn't me who killed Zeke! It was a woman from down the row. He'd been messing with her and she was mad at him. I swear!"

The figure stopped. A moment later a match flared, rose, and touched the end of a cigar. The light illuminated the face.

It was Joe Parlee.

When the cigar was lighted, Parlee approached and held the match up to show her face.

"Well, well! I thought it sounded like you. Nora, ain't it? Imagine us meeting here like this."

"Mr. Joe? Is it you? You ain't going to hurt me, are you?"

"Hurt you? Why would I want to do that?"

"Because of what Jimmy McCutcheon did. He hit you. He shouldn't have done that, Mr. Joe. He really shouldn't have. I didn't want him to."

Joe Parlee laughed, shaking out the match. "You didn't want him to, even though I'd just called you a whore?"

"I didn't mind it. I don't care what you say. I like you. I've always liked you, sir."

She felt his hand reach out and caress her

shoulder. "I well remember how you showed how much you liked me that time. A good memory. Don't worry, Nora. I ain't going to hurt you. I can't make the same promise for your partner, though. I didn't appreciate being struck. It ain't good for a man's pride, you know, and I've got as much as the next gent."

"He ain't my partner no more. He never really was. He'd murdered my husband back in Denver, and forced me to come with him."

"Just a minute ago you were babbling on that it was some woman who did it."

"I was lying, Mr. Joe. I was scared, and thought you was the law. It was Jimmy McCutcheon who done it, I swear."

"Where is he now?"

"Back in Marrowbone. Not the Marrowbone we were in this morning, but the other one."

"I see. And you escaped him."

"To tell you the truth, Mr. Joe, he was took away from me. By lawmen, I think. They came upon him while I was hid, and forced him away with them."

The flare of Parlee's cigar brightened and dimmed. She smelled the strong reek of acrid smoke against her face.

"Lawmen, you say?"

"I'm just guessing, that's all."

"I guess different. I don't think it was law. I

believe my dear brothers might be holed up in Marrowbone. Maybe it was some of their men."

"I wouldn't know that, sir. But I'll do all I can to help you get Jimmy McCutcheon, if you want. You can kill him for what he did, if you want to. I don't care none about him. I hate him, in fact." Just now Nora would say anything to ingratiate herself to Joe Parlee. She was a woman who was loyal, ultimately, only to herself, and if helping Joe Parlee find McCutcheon would benefit her, she'd do it without any hesitating.

"I'd be glad to find this McCutcheon. But I'd like to find my brothers a lot more."

"I don't know nothing about them," she said. "If I did, I swear I'd tell you."

"I believe you would, Nora. I sure do." He carressed her shoulder again, stepping closer. The cigar rolled from one side of his mouth to the other, and she tried to avoid coughing from the thick smoke that poured out of Joe Parlee's mouth.

"Think I'll keep you with me for a spell, Nora. What would you think of that?"

"I'd like that, Mr. Joe. I've liked you a lot ever since we were together." The fact was she despised him, just as she despised every man who'd paid her husband for the use and abuse of her body. But Nora told the truth only when it benefitted her.

"We got some extra mounts back here. We'll fetch you one."

"Have you got any food? Jimmy McCutcheon never would feed me. He was awful mean to me."

"I've got some food. You can eat it while you ride."

"Where are we going?"

"Into Marrowbone to pay a social call on my brothers."

Chapter Thirty-two

Penn was within fifty feet of the church when he heard the approach of someone from around the front corner. Caught in the open, he could only turn and run for the nearest cabin, another empty structure, a leftover from the older days of Marrowbone.

Penn hoped that somehow he'd moved quickly enough to avoid detection, but when he looked out a window of the cabin, past the broken shutter, he saw a man with a pistol drawn, darting up the slope, right in his tracks.

Penn moved back deeper into the cabin, drawing his pistol. But he didn't want to shoot; it would draw attention and attract other gunmen.

Penn had no time to make any alternative plan. The man was almost upon the cabin. Penn readied himself.

The man didn't appear. The doorway through

which Penn had expected to see him come remained empty.

Confused, Penn looked warily around, wondering if maybe he hadn't been seen coming in here after all. A few moments later, he holstered his pistol and breathed a sigh of deep relief.

The man struck from behind. Not in a hail of gunfire, but a full, bodily attack, with a knife glinting, ready to plunge as the man's other arm crooked around Penn's neck and choked down hard.

Penn groped for his pistol, then realized that he'd never get it into position to fire before that blade entered his heart. So he grabbed at the hand holding the knife instead, and wrestled with it. Penn was able to force the hand behind him, turning it. . . .

He shoved himself backward, and heard the man grunt strangely, spasm from head to toe. The arm with a chokehold on Penn's neck went weak and fell away.

Penn pulled away, turning, whipping out his pistol.

The man was standing there, his own knife jammed deep into his side. When Penn had pushed back, he'd done it at just the right moment to cause the man to stab himself. The man, dying on his feet, pitched forward, facedown.

Penn left the cabin with the dead man's pistol beneath his belt, his knife in his pocket.

Thunder rumbled and lightning flashed relatively close. It reminded Penn of that storm the night he so unexpectedly met Jim McCutcheon.

The flare revealed the town, and armed men moving through it. But at the moment, there was no one between Penn and the church. He ran across the clearing, knelt beneath a window, then lifted his head and looked through a crack in the shutter.

The church was occupied by ten or so hostages, a couple of nervous-looking gunmen guarding them. On the floor lay two bodies, one shot through the forehead, the other with his head smashed in as if by a club. Penn was shocked to see this sight. Who were the dead men? What had happened to them?

Something was going on inside. An old man and one of the gunmen were exchanging words, anger growing on both sides. Penn winced. *Sit down, old fellow. He'll kill you, if you make him mad enough.*

The gunman was swearing loudly, threatening the old man as others in the group either cringed away, or pleaded with the old fellow— Penn heard him called by the name "Welch"— to desist from antagonizing the guard. Penn hoped that Welch would listen, but doubted he would. He seemed a stubborn old fellow.

The gunman had had enough. He drew back his shotgun and tried to butt the old man in the face. Welch dodged it, but fell. The gunman raised the shotgun and leveled it.

Penn's pistol was already out, aimed through the hole.

He fired just before the gunman could squeeze the trigger. The man screeched and fell to the side, bleeding. He rolled over and writhed, then lay still.

The other guard, now alone in the church, stood stunned, staring at the shutter through which the shot had come.

He raised his own shotgun and reduced the shutter to splinters, but by then Penn was down, ducking well below the level of the window, having anticipated the guard would fire.

Penn came up again, aimed through the window, and looked for an opportunity for another shot at the second guard. But people were too close; he couldn't risk hitting a bystander.

Penn turned and ran, making other plans very quickly. He headed for the same abandoned cabin in which his unfortunate attacker had died on his own blade.

He knew the guard in the church could see him, so he dodged to the right the moment he anticipated the man taking another shot. It was a well-timed, well-directed move. The ground beside him was torn up by shotgun pellets, but Penn himself was untouched.

He ran into the cabin.

Moments later, the gunman from the church came running around the front of the building, shouting for others to join him. And one did. Another searching gunman, having also seen Penn, was racing up the slope from a different direction toward the cabin.

Inside the cabin, Penn saw them approach through a vacant window, and grinned.

"Knew you fellows couldn't resist the temptation."

Penn was on his knees, scrambling fast to complete his task. Timing would be very important for what he had in mind.

The gunmen reached the cabin at the same moment, paused on either side of the empty doorway, then both lunged inside.

They saw a man on the floor in the back of the cabin, lying very still. Was the black fellow pulling some kind of trick on them, playing 'possum?

They approached slowly, guns ready. The body didn't move. One nudged it with his foot.

"Look there! It's Park Everhart!"

The dynamite, its fuse burned almost completely down, came through the rear window and landed just beside the corpse. The gunmen, startled and confused, stared at it for a moment.

It was a moment they couldn't afford. By the time the realization of what it was came, and they were scrambling for the doorway, it was too late.

The fuse gave a final flare, and burned down to its end.

Out on the far outskirts of Marrowbone, Joe Parlee jerked his horse to a sudden halt at the explosion. It was some distance away, but still remarkably loud.

Nora, stuffing trail food into her mouth nearby, was so startled she dropped her cold biscuit and almost choked on the dry jerky she was trying to swallow.

"What the hell was that?" Joe Parlee asked.

"Sounded like dynamite," said the rider closest to him.

"What the hell's going on in that damned town?" Joe asked.

"Sounds like they're blowing each other up," the man answered.

For Marcus Parlee, the blast was much nearer, deafeningly loud, shaking the cabin in which he lay.

He shot up in the bed, swearing, then yelled in pain at the sudden movement.

Rosalita ran in from the next room, her face showing her terror.

"What was that, Marcus?"

"I don't know." He winced as he swung his legs out of bed. "I intend to find out, though. Bring me my pants. And my gunbelt."

"Marcus, no! You're in no condition for it!"

Outside, one of the two guards at Marcus's cabin door yelled as if he'd been stung.

"Go see what it is," Marcus ordered, stumbling across the room, reaching for his trousers.

Rosalita, knowing better than to argue with him, went back into the main room.

The door flew open, and one of the guards burst inside, looking like he'd just stared death in the face.

"It hit me!" he said, shuddering visibly. "It fell from the sky! It hit me right in the face!"

"What?" she asked.

He pointed through the door.

Just outside it lay a torn, severed human arm, bloody and still twitching.

Rosalita turned away, struggling against a sudden impulse to faint.

Chapter Thirty-three

W*ell,* Penn thought, *it was gruesome, but it worked. Four of them dead now. One stabbed in the cabin, one shot in the church, and two blown to pieces and raining all over Marrowbone.*

He wondered what Fitz St. John had thought when he heard the blast. Probably the oversized hermit was perched somewhere in his dark house, watching the tumult in Marrowbone through one of his peepholes.

The church was emptying now. Unguarded, the people ran free, scattering in all directions, heading for the outer edges of darkness and safety. Penn, hidden now among some boulders at the edge of the hill, watched them and mentally urged them on. *Get to where they can't find you, people. Stay out of sight, and leave the rest to me.*

He looked for McCutcheon among the scattering group, but saw no sign of him. He hoped that hadn't been McCutcheon's body on the floor of the church with half his head crushed. Because of the vicious mangling, it had been difficult to make out what the man would have looked like in life.

Penn pulled out a second stick of dynamite and began readying it, his mind working furiously. There were still gunmen moving about the town; he could see them each time lightning flared.

More outlaws meant more work for him to do, with his rifle, pistol, and St. John's old dynamite.

Nathan Parlee was on his knees, breathing hard, eyes wide, stunned by the force of the blast that had blown apart the empty cabin and sent wood, grit, and human bodies flying. He'd been so close that the concussion had knocked him off his feet.

Nathan, who'd left the church determined to lead the manhunt, had done little more than cower in the darkness, his nerve beginning to fail him. The blast had shattered what little fragment of courage he had left.

He knew the church was empty now. He'd seen the people, unguarded, fleeing from it. He felt no impulse to try to round them up again, which would be impossible, anyway. He just wanted to get away.

He checked his weapons and headed for the cabin where Marcus was.

He had no pride now. No ambition for leadership. Nathan Parlee needed his big brother.

But Marcus was not to be found. His cabin was empty, the men who'd guarded it gone, Rosalita missing along with him. Nathan poked about the cabin, confused, then exited and felt his boot toe nudge at something on the ground.

He looked down, unable to see what he'd hit. Stooping, he peered closer, then yelled with shock when a lightning flash revealed the severed arm.

Nathan fell back swearing, then ran from the cabin at top speed. A few paces outside he got hold of himself and stopped, looking around, hoping no one had seen him in such a panic.

Where was Marcus? He'd been bedridden; had he found the strength to get up?

Maybe someone had taken him away . . . Joe?

Nathan was worried now. Maybe Joe and the segment of the gang that had remained loyal to him had arrived. Maybe they'd gotten their hands on dynamite.

Nathan stood there on the hillside, so uncertain about what was happening, and what he should do about it, that he literally didn't know where to turn.

Marcus was having a hard time of it, as Rosalita knew he would. He lacked the strength to do what he was attempting. He belonged in bed, not out roaming the night in a mining town where people ran about like ants from a crushed anthill. Confusion reigned.

"It's Joe," Marcus said, walking slowly, gripping his injured side. "It's damned old Joe, coming to try and kill me again."

"If it is, then there is nothing you can do but try to hide," she said. "You're too hurt and too weak to either run or fight. Please, Marcus, let me find you a place to rest."

"He'll find me, Rosalita. If he's here, there's no place to hide from him. He'll look in every corner, every hole, until he's found me."

"Marcus, you're about to collapse. There's a storm building, and danger all around us. I'll find a safe hiding place for us. Please, let me do it!"

"I can make it," he said. "I can take care . . . of . . . myself . . ."

His words trailed off and he slumped to one knee, nearly ready to faint. Rosalita held on to his other arm, not letting him completely fall. She looked around for the men who had been his guards, but they were gone. They'd deserted their posts right after that inexplicable explosion, and the fall of that severed arm. She cursed them for their disloyalty.

"I'm afraid . . . I might pass out," Marcus said.

Rosalita looked around, seeking a place for them to hide.

She spotted a doorway built into the recess of a hillside, like that of a root cellar. It was isolated, the nearest building being the strange, windowless and doorless structure that covered almost an entire hillside, and which Rosalita had assumed must be some sort of storage building.

A root cellar would not be the most ideal hiding place, but probably no one would search for them there. It would be as safe a spot as she could hope to find for the man she loved, and feared she would soon lose.

"Marcus, there is a place," she said. "It's not far. Can you find the strength to walk? The door . . . see it?"

"He looked up and nodded.

"Come," she said. "I'll bear most of your weight."

With effort, he came to his feet and leaned on her. She was much smaller than he, but she was determined and strong, and he found that with her help, he could indeed walk.

They moved through the night toward the door to the apparent root cellar as thunder blasted and lightning seared down from the sky.

In the midst of all the confusion in Marrowbone, no one was more confused than Jim McCutcheon.

His heart was hammering, his mind rather numb, his consciousness not quite able to take in the fact that he'd killed a man.

It was justified; that he knew. Yet it had felt terribly like murder when he'd jumped the man guarding him, wrenched that shotgun away, and pounded the fellow's skull as hard as he could. Then he'd pounded him again and again, and when he looked at him next, he saw that he was most assuredly dead, his head actually caved in from the force of McCutcheon's blows.

With a great sense of unreality overwhelming him, McCutcheon had taken the man's weapons and fled the church before even the first of the hostages had returned from the privy line.

From then on, everything had gone very strangely.

McCutcheon had escaped in order to find some way to rescue the captives, but he'd not had the slightest notion of what to do. He'd hidden, tried to think, but achieved nothing.

Then came shooting down by the church, and

minutes later, that explosion, turning one of the empty cabins into shards of splintered wood.

Now there were no hostages left to rescue. The church was empty, the former prisoners scattered and hidden.

McCutcheon thought that maybe he should simply make a wide circle around Marrowbone, get out of town, and leave. But there was still the issue of Nora and Jake Penn.

McCutcheon was presently hidden high up in a field of boulders overlooking Marrowbone on the same side of town as the church. He was armed with the belted pistol and shotgun he'd taken from the guard he'd killed, but he'd not used either.

I'm useless, he thought. *I've killed a man so I could escape and rescue these folks, and now there's nobody to rescue.*

But there were still gunmen on the prowl, moving through the town, looking, Jim was sure, for him.

And maybe also for whoever had set off that dynamite blast.

He saw a man moving in the shadows down lower in the field of boulders, right at the edge, only yards back from a row of other ramshackle miner cabins. One of Parlee's gunmen, McCutcheon supposed.

McCutcheon readied the shotgun to fire, if

need be, and watched the man closely. He was up to something, fumbling about. McCutcheon saw a flare of light low to the ground, like a match had been struck.

Just then he noticed two Parlee gunmen creeping between two of the miner cabins; they'd seen the man, too.

That flare of light began to spark and brighten. McCutcheon watched as, through a gap between boulders, the hidden man eyed the approaching gunmen. He kept the flaring object low and hidden, then he rose and threw it. McCutcheon watched, stunned, as what appeared to be a stick of lit dynamite arced through the air, falling between the two cabins and almost squarely between the two sneaking gunmen.

It was a perfectly timed throw. The gunmen had just yelled in comprehension and turned to run when the dynamite exploded, sending them flying and demolishing much of both cabins. The roar of the blast faded in tandem with a long rumble of thunder.

Out across the town, shouts rose; men appeared on the lightning-illuminated streets, running toward the scene of this second explosion.

The man who'd thrown the dynamite turned to find his way out of the rocks. He froze when he saw McCutcheon's form rise before him farther up in the boulders, then reached for a pistol stuck in his belt.

"No need for that, Jake Penn," McCutcheon said. "I'm on your side, old friend."

"Jim? Jim McCutcheon?"

"It's me. Come on—they're coming up the hill, and we'd best get away from here, unless you've got more dynamite ready to throw."

"I got some, but I ain't ready to throw it. Good to see you, Jim."

McCutcheon moved through the boulders and joined Penn, and together they moved, crouched and hidden, through the boulder field, out on the other side, and away into the darkness.

Chapter Thirty-four

When they were far enough away to feel safe, they took refuge in a stand of evergreens and shook hands, slapping each other's shoulders.

"Good Lord, son, what brought you here?" Penn asked.

"I found Nora, Jake. I thought I did, anyway . . . now I'm not sure it's her. I knew you were coming to the high towns, so I sniffed out your trail and followed it."

"You *found* her? You went looking?"

"No, no. I didn't. I just stumbled across her. But Jake, I don't know if it's her."

"But it might be?"

"It might be."

"Dear Lord . . . where is she?"

"I don't know. She was hidden when I was taken prisoner by a couple of Parlee's men. I haven't seen her since and don't know what became of her. They never brought her in prisoner, though, so I don't think they've found her."

Penn stared off into the dark, thinking about it.

After a silence, McCutcheon said, "Jake . . . I killed a man. I hit him in the head with the butt of this very shotgun and killed him."

"It's an odd feeling, huh?"

"Yes."

"I know what you mean. I've killed several this evening."

"Killed killers. You and me both."

"But it still ain't natural."

"If it was, I suppose it would make us no different than the Parlees and their gang."

"That's right." Penn looked out of the trees over the town. "Rat-killing. That's what we've been doing."

McCutcheon nodded. "And there's still some rodents running around. How much of that poison you got left?"

Penn looked beneath his coat. "Five sticks."

"Let's go get some more rats, then. And find Nora, so you can tell me if I've brought you your sister, or gone through all this for nothing."

Penn smiled and nodded. "Let's go."

* * *

Marcus sat on the floor in the root cellar, and leaned back against the wall with his eyes closed. Rosalita had found a few candle stubs on the shelves, and had lighted a couple of them. In the flickering light, Marcus looked pale and sick, and Rosalita worried that the exertion had to hurt him severely.

She feared he would die, and there were tears in her eyes as she watched him.

There'd been another explosion just moments ago, out there somewhere. It had startled her, made her jump, but Marcus had only groaned and stirred, not even opening his eyes.

She prayed, *Dear God, don't let him die. He is a wicked man, God, I know he is, but I love him. I love him.*

Weeping, she leaned back against the rear wall of the cellar. It moved slightly.

Rosalita turned, surprised. She picked up one of the candle stubs and held it close to the wall.

She began to explore the wall with her hands, and in moments, had discovered what Penn had—the lever that opened the false wall. Once she figured out how to open the secret door, the blackness of the tunnel revealed itself to her.

Rosalita stood amazed. What was this place? Where did the tunnel lead? It seemed to penetrate deep into the hillside . . . the same one covered by that odd, windowless and doorless house.

Maybe it wasn't doorless, really. Perhaps *this* was the door.

Rosalita was a curious woman, also a woman determined to find the safest place for her beloved Marcus.

If she could take Marcus back into this hidden tunnel, close the door again, and get him, if possible, into that secure, fortress-like house, he would be safer there than anywhere else.

She looked back. Marcus was still asleep. She could take a candle, explore the tunnel briefly, and return to him.

Cupping the candle in her hands, she entered the tunnel's dark mouth.

Nathan Parlee was heading out of town. He had no idea where Marcus was, even if he was still alive. He wasn't sure whether Joe was near, but suspected that he was behind these unexpected explosions.

He sensed that he had to get away from Marrowbone now, or maybe he'd never get away at all.

But he didn't want his men—no, never really his men, he admitted to himself, but Marcus's— to see him fleeing. Better, actually, to let them suspect he'd been killed in one of those blasts.

Maybe they'd think that was his arm lying up there by Marcus's cabin.

Lightning flashed, followed by thunder so loud that Nathan thought another dynamite blast had gone off. He realized that lightning had struck a tree not far from him; it flamed like a massive torch, sending smoke and flame high into the sky.

The rain began softly, but was likely to grow harder before long. Nathan began looking for shelter. It was dangerous, he'd been told, to be among trees when lightning was flashing, but he despised rain, and had waited out many a storm under trees, never with bad results.

He headed for the trees, then stopped when he saw riders approaching up the road. He knew at once who they were.

Joe had come.

Nathan felt two contrary impulses, one to go to Joe, declare he was glad to see him, and give him his allegiance. The other was to run, fearing that Joe would give him the same treatment he'd already given Marcus.

The latter impulse won out. Nathan darted to the right into the trees, crouching down and wondering if he'd been seen.

He began to breathe again only after Joe and his riders were past. He saw something odd about the processional: there was a black woman riding with the band. He wondered who she was.

Nathan felt something brush his hip. He reached down, and found the sheath that held his knife empty.

"What the . . ."

She was right behind him. He fell as he tried to turn and rise at the same time.

Ginny Mason, who'd just slipped the knife from his belt, raised it and said, "You murdered my husband. You killed my son. Now I'll murder you."

He didn't even have time to scream before the knife came down.

Marcus Parlee opened his eyes. Rosalita knelt before him, her pretty face bathed in candlelight.

"Marcus, I've found a place that's safe. There's a tunnel here and it leads back into a house, a safe one. I went into it. It's empty. Do you have the strength to come with me?"

Marcus's tongue felt thick. "I'm hurting, Rosalita. I'm weak."

"Marcus, there's great danger outside. I want to take you to a safer place."

The exterior door to the root cellar shuddered on its hinges as another stick of dynamite exploded outside. Marrowbone had just lost one more "rat" who infested it.

Rosalita pulled on Marcus's arm. "I know you are weak, but I can take you where no one can find you."

"Joe . . . Joe is out there. Joe has dynamite."

"I don't know. Maybe. Please, Marcus, find the strength to go in with me."

With her help, he struggled to his feet. With a candle lighting their way, they entered the dark tunnel. Marcus suffered with every step, but she encouraged him. She had him wait, leaning against the tunnel wall, while she closed the false back of the root cellar again, enclosing them fully in the tunnel. Then they went on together.

Chapter Thirty-five

Penn and McCutcheon, hidden among the cabins of Marrowbone, watched nine riders entering the town in the rain. The newcomers seemed oblivious to the storm—all but one.

McCutcheon reached over and grasped Penn's arm. "Jake, that's Joe Parlee leading that band. And in the back, that's her!" He pointed at one of the riders near the rear of the group, the only one who was not visibly armed, the only one who was female, and the only one who was trying, vainly, to somehow duck away from the rain. "That's Nora!"

He felt Penn tense, sensed the man straining to get a good look at her through the rain and darkness. The quick flashes of lightning weren't enough to very effectively illuminate the woman, with her head down and shoulders up against the storm.

Joe Parlee pulled his horse to a halt, staring

at a gaping hole in the road. It was the crater left behind by Penn's most recently tossed stick of dynamite.

Joe raised his head, looking around the town, which now seemed empty. The people who had been held hostage in the church were now long gone, perhaps watching from hiding, perhaps simply hiding and not watching at all. The Parlee gunmen who had been their captors and guards were now gone as well, either killed by Jake Penn's dynamite, or hiding or fleeing themselves, into the mountains all around, less afraid of wilderness and storm than of the hell that had broken loose in Marrowbone.

None of this, though, Joe Parlee knew. He looked around the ghost town and called out loudly, "Marcus! Where are you, brother? I've come to talk to you!"

Within the dark St. John house, Marcus Parlee, seated weakly against a wall, lifted his slumped head, frowning. He looked at Rosalita. "Did you hear . . ."

"I heard nothing," she said quickly, knowing he would not remain still if he knew the brother who had shot him was outside, calling him. "Please, Marcus, sleep. Rest. You must heal."

"Marcus!" the cry came again, and this time there was no denying it. "Answer me, brother!

I've been tracking you! I know you're here, Marcus!"

Marcus pushed himself to his feet. He hardly had the strength to do it; only will born of anger gave him the power. "I'll not hide away from him, Rosalita. I can't do that."

She begged him to remain still, but he shook his head, pushing himself up despite the terrible, searing pain it generated inside him. He knew he was reopening the gunshot wound that had only just started to heal, but he went on, teetering on his feet and reaching for his pistol.

"Where's . . . the windows?" he asked, voice weaker. "I'll shoot Joe . . . out of his saddle. Just like he shot . . . me."

"I don't think there are windows, Marcus," she answered. "No windows, no doors . . . I don't know what this place is, but it's safe, if you'll only rest! Be quiet, and Joe will go away."

"No windows . . . no doors . . . what the hell kind of place is this?"

The room was lit only by two flickering candles. In the darkness beyond the twin spheres of light, something moved.

Marcus wheeled, hurting himself all the more. "Who's there?" he demanded. "Who is it?"

No one answered. But it had been no illusion; Rosalita had seen it, too.

Marcus raised the pistol, leveling it at the darkness. "I'll kill . . . you . . ."

The shadow within the shadows moved again with a shuffling noise, like a ghost fading away back into the blackness.

Marcus never fired. He swayed on his feet a few seconds, mouth open. A little line of drool escaped his lip, followed by another, then another, each one stained darker pink than the one that preceded it.

"I think . . . I've ruined myself," he said.

He collapsed to the floor at Rosalita's feet. She gasped, dropped to her knees, and placed her hand on his neck. No pulse. No breath. Marcus Parlee was dead.

Rosalita tilted back her head and screamed.

Joe Parlee turned his head toward the big, dark structure sprawled across the hillside.

"You hear that?"

"I did," said Graham Cooley, Joe Parlee's most loyal gunman. "It came from that dark house there."

"House? A warehouse is more what it looks like to me. Sounded like Rosalita, didn't it?"

"It sure did."

"Why you reckon she'd scream like that?"

"I don't know. Let's go in and find out. If she's in there, then Marcus will be, too."

He paused. "I don't see no door," Cooley said.

Joe studied the face of the building as lightning flashed. "Neither do I." He ordered two of his men to dismount and approach the house, looking for an entrance.

"I'm wet!" Nora whined. "I'm afraid of the storm! Please, Mr. Joe, let me go somewhere out of this rain!"

"Somebody shut that whore up," Joe said. "Marcus!" he shouted toward the St. John house. "You in there, brother?"

Silence.

"What's wrong? You a coward now? I want to talk to you, Marcus. About some money I'm due. Let's just talk, you and me." He paused. "Or do I have to burn this place down around your ears? I'll burn this whole town, if I have to!"

Inside the house, Rosalita picked up Marcus's pistol and stared at it in the candlelight. A cold, angry grief settled over her. The unseen thing, or person, or presence that had stirred in the darkness, whatever it had been, was unimportant now, nearly forgotten. Marcus was dead, and nothing else mattered.

Outside, Joe continued to harangue. Rosalita heard the noises of men moving outside the walls. She knew what they were doing. They were trying to find a doorway where there was none.

She held the pistol in both hands and looked down at the body of the man she loved. She knelt and kissed his whiskered cheek.

She then picked up a candle and headed back through the house the way she'd come, tears in her eyes and the pistol swinging at her side.

"So what now?" McCutcheon whispered. "Do we wait? Hope they'll go away?"

"Not with Nora so near," Penn whispered back. He paused. "Why is she with a band of outlaws? Why did he call her . . . what he did? A whore?"

It was not the time or circumstance in which McCutcheon could hope to answer those questions.

The rain began to slacken, and as Joe Parlee's men continued their vain search for an entrance into the St. John house, it died away altogether. Depleted, the clouds broke and the moon shone out. The night was nearly over now, but danger remained in Marrowbone as long as Joe Parlee did.

The truth of this was illustrated a moment later when, scared out of hiding behind a nearby smokehouse, one of the former hostages from the church appeared, making a panicked run across the road. McCutcheon recognized him from his limp; a man named Driscoll, he thought. One of the few holdover miners from Marrowbone's past days of glory.

"Will! Lonzo!" Joe Parlee barked.

Penn and McCutcheon watched as two of Parlee's men turned their horses after the fleeing man. They overtook him easily, one of them dragging him down from the saddle. The other dismounted and joined the first, helping pin Driscoll to the ground beneath his boot.

"Just an old fellow!" he hollered over to Parlee.

"Please!" Driscoll pleaded loudly. "Please let me go! I've done nothing to you!"

"What do you want to do with him, Joe?" the second gunman called.

"I got no use for him," Parlee said. "It's Marcus I want."

"You'll let me go?" Driscoll said tentatively.

"Run along, old fellow," one of his captors said.

Driscoll rose, smiling a little at his good fortune, and began limping away down the road.

Parlee gave a quick nod. Both gunmen drew pistols, took aim, and shot him down as he walked.

Nora screamed and turned her face away.

Laughter coursed among the outlaws.

"There's one who'll not go running off and bringing trouble back to us," Joe Parlee said.

Penn looked at McCutcheon. "No mercy, Jim," he whispered. "Not to a one of them. That was cold murder right there."

"I can't find no door, Joe!" called one of the men who'd circled the house twice, looking for an entrance. "There just ain't none! Nor a single window."

"Hell, there's got to be!" Parlee said and dismounted. "Rosalita's in there. I heard her. I know that voice. Everybody look for an entrance! There's no house that don't have some way to get into it."

"What kind of place is that, anyway?" McCutcheon whispered to Penn.

"It's a house built by a crazed man named St. John. He's dead now, but his son is still inside. I've been inside myself, earlier on."

"There's a woman in there, too. I heard her."

"So did I. I can't explain that."

"So where's the door?"

"Tunnels, Jim. Tunnels. One of them behind a false wall in that root cellar over there. There's another leading out into some woods, and maybe a third one as well."

"There's a story to be told here, I take it."

"Yes. No time to tell it, though."

"Penn, if they come together in a group again, a well-thrown stick of dynamite—"

"No. Not with Nora so near."

Nora, of all those who had ridden in, was the only one who had remained mounted. Now, though, she climbed down from her horse and began walking toward the far side of the road.

One of the Parlee men noticed her. "Where are you going?"

"I think I'm going to get sick," she said. "You shot down that man! You killed him!"

"You stay where you are," the outlaw told her.

Something fell from beneath her coat, dislodged when she climbed off her horse, and thudded at her feet.

"What's that?" the gunman asked.

"Nothing," she said. "Nothing." She kicked at it, scooting it behind her.

But he was approaching, looking closely. "Dynamite?" he said tentatively. "It *is*!" He shouted, "Joe! Come here! She's got a damned stick of dynamite!"

The entire band of outlaws came running, so near to where Penn and McCutcheon hid that they very nearly stepped upon them.

Chapter Thirty-six

Joe Parlee held the stick of dynamite gingerly, then looked up at Nora's frightened-looking face. "Where'd you get this?"

"I found it."

"Found it. Where?"

"In a room, off the side of a tunnel."

"A mine, you mean?"

"I guess. I don't know. I just found it and took it because I didn't have no weapon."

"What about a fuse and detonator?"

She produced them.

Joe grinned, then turned to the dark house. "Hey, Marcus! You best stand back—we're coming in!"

"Oh, no," Penn whispered as he watched them proceed with what was very evidently a plan to blow their way into the building. "Poor Fitz. And anybody else who may be in there. I hope he's far away from where they place that stick."

"Who's Fitz?"

"The son of that crazed man I mentioned. A little crazed himself, actually. But an innocent sort of fellow. I hate to think what they'll do to him when they find him in there."

"Any way to get him out?"

Penn thought hard, looking over the situation. Parlee and all his men were occupied setting the dynamite, most of them out of sight around a corner of the house. Only Nora remained out on the road. If Penn and McCutcheon moved, she'd see them. How she'd react was impossible to say.

But Penn couldn't sit by and risk letting Fitz be killed in such a way. The idea was intolerable.

"I got to do something, Jim. Got to take a risk, for the sake of an innocent man. No time to explain. Can I trust Nora not to react if she sees me?"

"What? I don't know! You mean you're going to—"

"I am. Here, take this and use it if you have to." He handed McCutcheon a stick of dynamite, with the detonator and fuse already in place. "Got matches?"

"Yes."

"Good."

Penn rose, coming out of his hiding place and moving down to the road. Nora saw him in the moonlight. Her eyes widened, her hand rose slightly, and her lips parted—but he motioned to her for silence, then beckoned for her to come.

She looked very scared, her eyes unblinking and flicking back and forth between the preoccupied outlaws and Penn.

He beckoned again. She hesitated, then approached.

She passed near him, pausing for a second, looking into his face, and he into hers.

"Jake? Jake Penn?" she asked in the tiniest of whispers.

"Yes," he said. "It's me."

She nodded, then ran on to hiding. Penn sneaked over to the root cellar door, opened it, and went inside. He swung open the false wall and plunged into the tunnel without the benefit of light.

Scraping the wall, tripping, bumping himself in every way possible, he hurried down the tunnel, passing the room where two members of the St. John family lay entombed, and entered the true cellar of the house. He scuffed through the unseen pile of letters written by a man to his dead wife, and up the stairs to the upper level of the house.

"Fitz!" he called in a loud whisper. "Fitz! Where are you?"

"I'm here." Fitz's voice was tremulous and thin. "I'm over here . . . I hit her—I wasn't trying to hurt her. She was going to go outside and shoot someone, I think. I knew they'd kill her. I had to stop her so they wouldn't. I don't like it when people are killed."

"We'll all be killed if we don't get out of here," Penn said. "Those men out there are about to blow a hole in these walls with dynamite so they can rush in. Hurry! We've got to get into the tunnels."

"The tunnels?"

"The blast won't reach you there. And you can escape while they're searching through the house."

"I'm afraid to leave here!"

"You must! You'll die otherwise. So will she. Pick her up, Fitz. Let's go. Now!"

There were no lights burning in the house, but Penn could tell by sound alone that Fitz was obeying him, however hesitantly. "You take her down the root cellar tunnel," Penn directed. "When you hear the explosion, take her outside. Go up among the empty cabins and hide. Get as far as you can away from this house. Do you understand? As far as you can! I'll join you later, very soon."

"Where will you go?"

"Into a different tunnel. Now hurry. Please. And be careful."

"What are you going to do?"

"I'm going to see if I can't rid this town of the last of the rats who've infested it," Penn replied. "Now go! Quickly!"

He couldn't worry further about Fitz, nor about the woman, whoever she was. Rosalita, someone outside had called her. An associate in some way of this large outlaw band, obviously. The details didn't matter right now.

Penn crossed the house in the darkness, no easy task for him as it would have been for Fitz, who knew the place so well.

He could hear Joe Parlee's men working outside, up against the house, close to where he was. The explosion could come at any moment.

He reached the door leading down to the tunnel off of which the dynamite was stored. He tried to open it, but found it to be jammed. Penn almost panicked.

"We'll be in real soon, Marcus!" Joe Parlee's voice chortled from outside. "Best stand back!"

Penn rammed the door with his shoulder, hard, once, then twice.

It opened.

He sprang into the tunnel, scrambling, running. He would be safe now from the blast, if it should come in the next few moments, but there was more to his plan than simple escape.

He reached the door of the explosives room and opened it. Only a fraction of the dynamite had been removed. Penn grabbed a half-filled box, picked it up, and ran back down the tunnel with it.

He carried it up to the door he'd rammed open to exit the house. Placing it there, he pulled from his coat the final stick of dynamite out of the supply he'd gathered before. He fitted it with a detonator and a fuse and placed the stick in the midst of the other sticks in the box.

He went back down the tunnel, stringing the long fuse out as he went.

McCutcheon had been surprised and somewhat confused when he saw the root cellar door open and a very fat, long-haired man come waddling out, bearing in his arms the unconscious body of a beautiful Mexican woman. He scurried with her up toward the empty cabins.

Nora saw him, too, and stared in amazement.

Some instinct spoke to McCutcheon, and he rose. "Nora!" he called, just loud enough for her to hear. "Come here!"

"Jimmy?"

"Shhh! Don't let them know! Come here, to me!"

She looked uncertain, glancing toward the place where the Parlee men were getting ready to set off the stick of dynamite she'd provided them. But then she moved, running toward McCutcheon.

"Jimmy . . . don't let them do nothing bad to me!"

"I won't," he said. "Come on. Let's move up farther, away from them."

"Is Jakey here?"

"Not here," McCutcheon said. He pointed toward the St. John house. "In there."

Jake Penn was running through the tunnel when the blast of Joe Parlee's single stick of dynamite jarred the house and sent grit falling down upon him from above.

The door into the tunnel he occupied hurtled open from the force of the explosion, which had, as intended, knocked a large opening through one of the exterior walls. The door knocked the box of explosives he'd placed back down the rough staircase, spilling its contents all around.

Penn had not counted on that happening, and wasn't sure he had time to correct it.

He hurried back, gathering as many of the sticks as he could feel, putting them back in the box, and again burying the fused stick in the midst of them.

Joe Parlee and his men, hooting and shouting, were pouring into the house. He heard them, and in moments he would see them.

No time . . . no time . . .

Penn bit the fuse short and threw aside the excess. He struck his last match and touched the slight fuse. It flared brightly.

He shoved the box through the doorway into the house, rolled back down the rocky stairs, then ran blindly through the tunnel toward its end.

When the St. John house exploded, McCutcheon was knocked back onto the ground, and Nora screamed like she'd been hit by lightning.

The blast was tremendous, bigger than any McCutcheon had ever seen. Almost the entire windowless building ruptured, the roof blowing clear off, the walls blowing outward, and Joe Parlee and every one of the men with him no doubt dying without ever knowing what had hit them.

McCutcheon covered his head as grit, wood shards, and assorted rubbish rained down amid sparks.

When at last it was over, McCutcheon sat up and looked at the rubble on the hillside. It was hard to tell that what was there had ever been a building. It was now only a shapeless heap of broken lumber and rising dust.

McCutcheon rose and stared at it, disbelieving. "Penn!" he whispered. "Oh, no. Penn."

Chapter Thirty-seven

Nora came to McCutcheon's side, just as stunned as he was.

"Are they dead?" she asked weakly.

"Yes. I think you can be sure that they are. I think Penn set off that blast. I think he meant to get them all at once."

"But what about him?"

McCutcheon was astounded at just how hard it was for him not to break into tears right now. He'd not imagined he'd gained such an affection for Jake Penn, a man he still didn't know all that well.

"I think it probably killed him, too," he managed.

As the sun rose over Marrowbone, the people of the town began to emerge from hiding. They came down the hillsides, weary and still looking scared, but knowing that, at last, it was over.

Several gathered around the body of Driscoll,

the last victim of the Parlees. Among that group, McCutcheon noticed, was Ginny Mason. She had a more peaceful expression than she had earlier. He wondered why.

Nora's hand groped out and grasped McCutcheon's arm suddenly. "Jimmy! Look!" She pointed.

Jake Penn was approaching. He was coming down the back yard behind the shattered St. John house, looking like a man about to fall over from exhaustion. He was dirty, gritty, his clothing black with smoke, but he was smiling and didn't seem to be hurt.

McCutcheon ran toward him. Nora remained behind.

McCutcheon hugged Penn unabashedly, pounding his back with the flat of his right hand. "Thank God!" McCutcheon said. "I thought you'd died, too."

"Not hardly," Penn replied. He looked across McCutcheon's shoulder at Nora. "Somebody I want to meet is standing over there, Jim," he said.

"Yes. Of course," McCutcheon replied. "Come on. Let's get this done."

Nora stood solemnly as Penn approached her. She did not shirk from his stare, and McCutcheon thought that at that moment she looked finer than he'd yet seen her. He could see how this abused, hardened woman might, in the right circumstances, be found to have some dignity and even beauty about her.

Penn stood silently, looking into her face. He smiled softly, the morning light bathing over him. "It's not you, is it," he said.

There were no lies now. Nora shook her head. "No, sir. It's not. I ain't your sister."

McCutcheon was disappointed, if not surprised. He'd dared hope that she would indeed prove to be Jake's long-lost sister.

"Why did you lie?" Penn asked.

"To get myself away from Denver, away from trouble," she said. "I didn't figure that you'd be able to know whether I was your sister or not, after so long a time. I figured I could lie my way through. Now . . . now I don't even want to lie. My name really is Nora . . . I just ain't *your* Nora." She paused, and said, "I truly wish I was."

Penn smiled at her. "I forgive you for lying," he said. "I think I can look at you and see that life's not been easy for you. You had your reasons for what you did, I suppose."

"I'm sorry," she said, and for the first time, McCutcheon had the impression that Nora was being nothing but utterly sincere.

The survivors of Marrowbone were now gathered in small groups, some weeping, others laughing, others looking merely stunned. The ruined St. John house was gathering much attention.

Penn looked about. "Where's Fitz?"

"Who?"

"Fitz St. John. The man who lived in the house there . . . while it still was a house."

"I saw him going up among the cabins, Penn. Carrying a woman."

"One of the Parlees' women, I believe," Penn said. "Come on. Let's go find him."

He'd already been found by the time they reached the place where Fitz had hidden himself. A man McCutcheon recognized from among the former hostages was kneeling near the pale, unshorn figure of Fitz St. John, who was curled into a fetal posture behind a smokehouse.

"Is he all right?" McCutcheon asked, extending his hand to the man, who shook it.

"I think so," the man said. "My name's Vernon Paxton. I know this young man. Knew his father a lot better. I'm surprised, though . . . I'd thought Fitz was dead."

"No," Penn said. "His father and brother are gone, but Fitz is very much still with us." He knelt and put his hand out, touching Fitz's shoulder. "Fitz, look at me. Look at me. It's Jake Penn."

Fitz lifted his face up. He was frightened, his skin fish-belly white from his life in the darkness, and his eyes squinted terribly in the morning light. But he looked relieved to see Penn.

"Where is the woman?" Penn asked.

"She woke up and ran away," he said. "I don't know where she went."

"Let her go, then," Penn said. "There's certainly nothing left for her here. Fitz, I had to destroy your house. I'm sorry."

"My house?"

"Yes. You heard the explosion, maybe saw it?"

"I heard it." He began to look panicked. "Where will I go? What will I do?"

Paxton said, "You've got a place with me as long as you need it, Fitz. Your father helped me out many a time. He was a man not many understood; I knew him better than most. He helped me, and now I'll help you."

Fitz looked at him, and nodded, then buried his face again, hiding from the unfamiliar light.

Two hours later, Penn and McCutcheon sat eating together, fed by the small but grateful populace of Marrowbone. They were both ravenous and ate voraciously.

"Nora's gone," Penn said when they'd eaten enough to allow them to think about something other than filling their bellies as fast as possible. "She slipped away about an hour ago. God only knows where she's going."

"That woman brought me a world of trouble," McCutcheon said. "She was no easy companion. I wouldn't have put up with her if I'd really known she wasn't your sister. I suspected that was the case, but couldn't be sure."

"I'll know my Nora when I find her."

"Where will you look now?"

Penn wiped his mouth on his sleeve. "I don't know. I'll start digging for new information. Find some new tracks and follow them."

McCutcheon laid down the half-loaf of bread he'd been gnawing on, and looked seriously at Jake Penn. "You ever think about taking on a partner?"

Penn grinned. "You got one in mind?"

"Just a drifter, a fellow who seems to find bad luck everywhere he goes. A fellow you keep having to dig out of one hole or another."

Penn grinned. "Just the kind of partner a man needs."

McCutcheon grinned back, extending his hand. They shook. "It's Penn and McCutcheon, then. For now. Until we find your Nora."

Jake Penn nodded. "Penn and McCutcheon it is."